SMIRT

An Urbane Nightmare

By Branch Cabell

SMIRT
SPECIAL DELIVERY
THESE RESTLESS HEADS

By James Branch Cabell

BIOGRAPHY OF THE LIFE OF MANUEL

SMIRT

An Urbane Nightmare

BY BRANCH CABELL

"He accepts that middle world in which men take no side in great conflicts, and decide no great causes, and make great refusals. He thus sets for himself the limits within which art, undisturbed by any moral ambition, does its most sincere and surest work."

WILDSIDE PRESS

Published by
Wildside Press, LLC
P.O. Box 301
Holicong, PA 18928-0301 USA
www.wildsidepress.com

Wildside Press Edition: MMIII

For

GEORGE JEAN NATHAN

Granting dullness might esteem
Egoistic any dream
Of an author's loves and laurels,
Rightly I recite its morals . . .

Gifted, Smirt forever finds
Everywhere inferior minds;
Jesting, Smirt provokes insanely
Each and all reared less urbanely;
And, derided, Smirt derides.

None the less, Smirt too decides
Neither wit nor erudition
Amply bolsters Smirt's position . . .

Thereupon, with heart unhurt,
He perceives that Smirt stays Smirt,
And attests this by imploring
Naught of dullness save ignoring.

* *

AUTHOR'S NOTE

*

This book attempts to extend the naturalism of
Lewis Carroll. That seems an explanation demanded
by honesty; and, in its turn, demanding a paragraph
or so to explain it.

In 1929, then, during the revising of *The Cream of
the Jest* into its definitive version, the thought occurred to the writer of *The Cream of the Jest* that,
with one striking exception, nobody had as yet published a dream-story combining any considerable
length with even the most shadowy pretence to veracity. Here and there one found a short story which,
in its stinted way, stayed veracious enough. Even in
The Cream of the Jest one found, among forty chapters, four chapters which seemed veracious. But Lewis
Carroll alone of mankind appeared to have written
books which dealt, and which dealt only, with the true
stuff of dreams; which covered entirely the course of
a normal dream; and which progressed at all times,

as a dream does normally progress, under the local regulations of dream land.

In *The Cream of the Jest* one considered—a bit ruefully—a novel builded about the dreams of a novelist. But one considered, also, the real issue dodged, and dodged doubly, by the facts: (*a*) that the dreams of Felix Kennaston were indicated by extracts or summaries; and (*b*) that these dreams were induced by extraneous means, more or less magical. Turning thence to *Jurgen*, to *The High Place*, to *Figures of Earth*, and to yet other volumes emanating at diverse periods from the same typewriter, one discovered, in very ample quantity, the dream which this or the other magic induced, and which (in consequence of a reason well known to all students of goetia) conformed to the logic, and to the touchstones, and to the experience, of a person who is awake. None of these volumes recorded any dream from the authentic, the wholly familiar standpoint of a normal dreamer. And it seemed odd that, after so much yearlong traffic with dreams, the author of the Biography of the Life of Manuel had never once dealt realistically with any more realistic species of dream.

Odder still seemed the fact that, when you came to think of it, there did not appear to exist in American literature, whether in its maturity or during its prolonged infancy in England, any full-length dream-story which obeyed the actual and well-known laws of a normal dream—with the ever-memorable exception of the two Alice books by Lewis Carroll. These books alone did preserve the peculiar, the unremittent movement of a normal dream, and the peculiar logic of a normal dream, and the peculiar legerdemain through which the people one meets, or the places visited, in a normal dream, are enabled unostentatiously to take visible form or to vanish, quite naturally, without provoking in the beholder's mind any element of surprise; just as these books preserved, too, the ever-present knowledge, common to many dreamers, that, after all, they are dreaming...But I forbear to particularize the true somnial touch with which matters are handled. My point is that, in 1929, these two books remained inexplicably unfellowed in our literature, as the sole known æsthetic instances— I believed—of an elaborate and unflinching naturalism applied to the lands beyond common-sense.

Even here the precise might file an objection. Alice smells pepper in Wonderland, she smells the "scented rushes" in Looking-Glass Land; and, upon several occasions, Alice partakes of food, and of physic also— tasting, as you may recall, an unusual medicine which had "a sort of mixed flavor of cherry-tart, custard, pineapple, roast turkey, toffy, and hot buttered toast." It is my strong personal belief that in no dream not

ix

induced by black magic or by gray magic did anybody ever smell or taste anything. So that small objection to the scientific exactness of Lewis Carroll is recorded in this place, for whatever it may be worth,—
with the glad supplement that in every other important respect one finds his books to be triumphs in
naturalism, with which the works of Flaubert, or of
Zola, or of Tolstoi, let us say, cannot easily be
compared.

*   *

*

Returning to *The Cream of the Jest*, it seemed in-
creasingly needful to the author of *The Cream of the
Jest*, during the months which he gave over to revising *The Cream of the Jest*, that some novelist other
than Lewis Carroll should treat a full-length dream,
at full length, realistically. The trend of the time,
one reflected, stayed definitely averse from any form
of too timid restraint such as continued to enslave our
creative writers. I mean (of course) that professed
realists had given us, very multitudinously, the stark,
the grim, and preferably the sex-flavored, truth about
man's life during his wideawake hours—the truth
about just two-thirds of human existence,—without

ever daring, it would seem, to venture beyond that rather vulgar fraction. All their novels displayed a quaint devotion to insomnia.

The eight hours, more or less, which every human being devotes to sleep appeared to repel the professed realist; to bother him, in some obscure fashion; and to be a theme which no realist cared, or perhaps had the courage, to handle. Dreams had been analyzed and interpreted, *ad,* as the learned say, *infinitum,* and even, the impatient append, *ad nauseam;* but never since 1871 had any English or American writer dealt with any complete and convincing dream completely and convincingly.

All this, too, in face of the plain fact that every normal person spends some third part of his existence in sleep, during which (according at least to such eminent authorities as Kant, Leibnitz, Descartes, and yet other reputable philosophers) every sleeper dreams continuously, and so, for eight hours *per noctem,* lives among supernatural surroundings and wields supernatural powers. Yet Lewis Carroll alone of our better-known realists had considered this huge field, this entire third of human life, with any seriousness or any veracity. And even this great pioneer had confined his explorings to the south temperate zone, as it were, in the callow, the sexless dreams of a child.

It followed that nowhere in English prose literature was an adult dream represented from the actual point of view of a dreamer; and that some thirty-three per cent. of human experience remained untouched by any living creative writer at all truthfully. Since Bunyan's time there had been an abundance of books which purported to record dreams; but, thus far, only two of them had tried honestly to obey the conditions of dream land, wherein all human beings pass a third of their lives.

It really did seem a default which ought to be remedied.

*   *

*

Here, in *The Cream of the Jest*, glimmered a fair starting point for that remedying. Caution whispered that to present the dreamer as one who lived as a littérateur during his waking hours would make it difficult for dullards to see in the proposed book anything save a re-writing of *The Cream of the Jest*. He could as easily be a painter, said caution, or, perhaps better still, a professional book reviewer; though indeed, for that matter, without any large difficulty, he could be made a stock broker, or a minister of the gospel (a notion with some fine possibilities), or a merchant, or a lawyer, or, yet more simply, a person of independent means. Such persons were still about in 1929. In brief, the sole needs of my protagonist as the tale shiftingly took form in 1929, seemed a fair allowance of literacy and of definite theories about art.

Ah, but then—as experience forthwith assured me —but if I did make my protagonist a professional writer, no dullard anywhere would be able quite to avoid the belief I was writing about myself; and as a further, most salutary consequence, no dullard would fail to be rather cordially irritated. (It is for this reason, I remark in passing, that I always incline to make my protagonist a writer, or at the very least a potential writer, just as I labor toward much the same end when I hyphenate Richmond-in-Virginia.) Thus did experience woo me, outwhispering caution, and sturdily prompting me not to remit the pleasures promised by a continuance in mock egotism. And to the sage voice of experience I hearkened most reverently, because at my age one knows experience to be the best teacher.

So, then, did experience lead me to decide that my protagonist, like Felix Kennaston (but, above all, like me, before my late conversion to naturalism) must perforce be a writer of romantic novels: and gradually my protagonist came closer toward me, solidifying, a little by a little, as it were, during his slow emergence from that shadowy realm in which the as yet uncreated characters of fiction abide restively; and he revealed to me, first of all, his inevitable name, his *mot juste*. After that, he revealed his dream, just as clearly as (but not a jot clearlier than) it had been revealed to him.

*   *

*

He revealed also, as I came to convert this dream into words and sentences and punctuation marks, an unpliant obstinacy. "But that," he would repeat, parrot-like, whensoever I attempted to touch up a bit improvingly his revealings, "that is not the way it was." And there was no doing anything with the man until I had returned meekly to his far less attractive version of the affair in hand. From the beginning to the end of his story (which was not the real end, to be sure, because a great deal else happened afterward) he has thus caused me endless trouble.

For my gradually evoked acquaintance insisted that

in this dream he had lacked not merely the ability to smell or to taste anything. His power of vision also was circumscribed, indescribably. Oh, yes, he saw everything clearly enough, in so far as went any practical need. It was only that a sort of mistiness pervaded matters, driftingly, unpredictably. And besides, at times, one or another visual detail would seize on the attention, obsessing it, somewhat as though, from a shrouding fog, this particular detail—an eyebrow, it might be, or a red note-book, or perhaps a horn snuff-box—had been picked out by a flashlight. In consequence, you did not ever obtain a leisured and complete view of any person or of any place.

It sounds trivial enough. Yet this was a limitation, I soon found, which debarred the higher reaches of picturesque writing, because upon no occasion had my protagonist seen quite enough of anything to afford me the material for an elaborate describing of it. There was, for the rest, no noticeable abatement, he reported, in hearing or in touch: but three of his senses were as though drugged, two of them completely, and the other in part.

Moreover, there was in his dream no perception of time. For the convenience of the reader I have suggested here and there a short interval of time, just as I have mercifully divided the book into chapters, to afford breathing spells. Yet here again has my friend

remarked dubiously, "But that is not the way it was."
For in point of fact, he declared, there were no intervals. Everything happened, as it were, simultaneously,
or at least almost simultaneously, now that events,
and many persons too, merged swiftly and unaccountably, but quite naturally, into yet other events, or
yet other persons; so that the action of this dream
could not be thought of as consuming any definite
period...There seemed, in so far as my reporting
dreamer could phrase the affair, to be no important
difference between the length of a minute and the
length of a century and the length of a yardstick, because time had become a matter incomprehensible
and remote. He did not any more travel through time,
but instead, time was now travelling about him, at a
varying and, in so far as he was concerned, an irrelevant gait...And space did very much the same
thing. He did not often go to any place in this dream,
for the sufficing reason that the place—swiftly and
unaccountably, but quite naturally—came to him.
He had severed, in brief, all his daylit relations with
time and space.

*   *

*

But I forbear to cite further the conditions of any normal dream, inasmuch as these conditions are familiar to all mankind. My point is merely that I have endeavored to conform to every one of these conditions, and have found them to be both hampering and stimulating, throughout this book.

I remark likewise that to write truthfully about human dreams is an enterprise, howsoever difficult, which I would recommend to my fellow realists, because their continued avoidance of an entire third of every human life seems to me a bit cowardly. Finally, I rejoice to have rectified, at least, and at howsoever long a last, my own delinquency in this matter.

Richmond-in-Virginia
October 1933

CONTENTS

xix

CONTENTS

CONTENTS

xxi

PART ONE

POINT OF DEPARTURE

* *

*

"*In describing Peter the Hermit, Gibbon says that 'his stature was small, his appearance contemptible; but his eye was keen and lively; and he possessed that vehemence of speech which seldom fails to impart the persuasion of the soul.' He had been a soldier, but is declared to have adopted a monk's robe in order to escape from an old and ugly wife.*"

ONE

*   *

AFTERNOON OF A VIRTUOSO

*

You lived in contentment. Your desired work was done. The romantic novels which you had written pleased, at all events, you. Sedately and wholly, as cool water contents a thirsting man, so did these books satisfy you, not because of their super-eminence in any special grace or profundity, but because they were what you had desired to do, and that which, somehow, amid all dissuasions, all stumbling-blocks, and all treacheries of chance, you had done. The completed novels thus figured, in your more frank moments of reverie, as a tangible prize, no more valuable in itself, perhaps, than a blue ribbon or a laurel wreath, but none the less as a tangible prize, in the prolonged game played against time and accident and one's own frailty.

For they were, whatever else they were, very much what you had desired them to be: they existed to-day in fair accord with your first, your now ancient, your

3

not ever stinted or altered design. At times it seemed to you that something more strong and more deeply rooted than you could quite imagine had willed these books to exist, making use of you, willy-nilly, as the makeshift to get them on paper; so that your true part, in the outcome, had been but little more pre-meditated than was the contribution of the people who had manufactured your carbon ink or your type-writer: but more frequently you elected to let com-placency lounge on a free stage, whensoever you re-garded those assembled and unique books in which, now, you had no further need, nor any real wish, to read.

"I prefer not to infringe," you said modestly, "upon posterity's privilege. Let us avoid *hubris*, that over-weening pride which destroyed Œdipus, and Prome-theus, and so many other protagonists of Greek drama."

Your books were done. They represented the prize gained from a prolonged contest in which you had been victorious. Yet they represented also the receipt for a debt honorably paid in full. For there had been, not merely the desire, but, in some sort, the obliga-tion likewise, to make these books, to make these books and no other books. Their corporeal existence thus contented alike your sense of thrift and your sense of honesty.

4

That was the main thing: the books were done, precisely as you had planned them. And upon less serious grounds also, you were content with life. Almost all your past had been—upon the whole—agreeable in the time of its being; and to recall it remained agreeable. The present had not any serious flaw. Your living, day by day, contented, at all events, you. Your home and your wife and your children appeared each to be a desirable enough example of such belongings. Your income sufficed. For the rest, you assumed tacitly that a certain amount of deference was due by all your associates; and from every one of them you received it.

You were thus a personage, to a reasonable extent. It was a fact which your intelligence could not, and did not ever attempt to, ignore.

"Nevertheless—" said the black dog.

And it rather startled you.

*   *

THE BLACK DOG

*

Nevertheless," said the black dog, "all these fine words and fine thoughts and these smug self-justifyings do not content Smirt."

It seemed odd at the time, because you had noted, with the trained perceptiveness of a professional writer, that dogs do not speak English ordinarily; and besides, this was a wooden dog, in which you kept stray bits of string. He was mostly black, but he had a white muzzle and four white feet; his back lifted off when you took hold of his white tail; and he stood on top of the radiator cover in your writing room, regarding the world without optimism. But that was not the immediate point.

"Do you tell me, black dog, who is Smirt? For I can think of no name more flippant or more contemptuous sounding, nor of any name which I like less."

"Smirt," said the black dog, "is Smirt."

"Thus far your logic is unassailable. Up to this point I follow your argument."

"And Smirt remains Smirt," the black dog continued, "no matter what else he may be called in the telephone book or in your press clippings or in the adoring babble of idiots; and you know very well whom I mean."

"That is perhaps true, black dog. None the less, there was once a princess. And I remember that, off and on, in a world wherein princesses are to be seen only on Sundays, as they figure unalluringly in the rotogravure sections of the New York papers. I remember there was once a princess, all-beautiful and all-wise, a witty and a tender princess, of whom there are no tidings in that strange world which the newspapers tell about in their commensurably strange language."

"Zero Weather," remarked the black dog, "Creeps South. Four Lives Claimed in Feud War, Five Wounded. Congress Meets in Heated Session."

"And of these matters, black dog, I would be the last to deny the importance. But my princess is more important."

"Rev. D. W. Cook," the black dog said, "Resigns as Pastor on Account of Health. French Cabinet Split. 8 Killed, 100 Injured, in Ohio Store Blaze.

This is How Doctors Treat Coughs and Colds. Threats of Ultimatum Loom."

"And what does that portend, black dog?"

"It means that you are imprisoned in a cheap and tawdry and hackneyed place, poor Smirt, in a place where many people do not appreciate your genius properly. You have not in this place your suitable audience."

"And yet, black dog, I am well enough content here."

"Is it possible for you to be contented, Smirt, anywhere that you do not matter? What matters in this place is that Worried Mother Slays Son & Self. County Sheriff Acquitted in Dry Law Case. Noted Painter Predicts End of Marriage Tie. On Saturdays Only You Can Get 10 Zip Razor Blades for 39¢ with This Coupon."

"But I do matter, black dog, for in a number of romantic novels I have made mirth and wonder and loveliness."

"Who cares about your makings? Who cares anywhere, except in the obscurity of literary supplements, and in the chaos of columnists, about Smirt? Only a few hundred or so thousand persons heed the judicial comments of this small civilized minority now that Biplane Plunges Near Golden Gate. A great many living people are not talking about Smirt at this very

8

moment. It is more important in this place that Masked Mob Forestalls Justice. Mild Losses Seen as Curb Closes. So-and-so Flayed in Quiz. Somebody Else Goes Jestingly to Death Chair. 43 Women's Dresses, Formerly to $16.50, Now $5.00."

"It is very true, black dog, that many newspapers do not review my books on the front page of the news section—which has always seemed to me a mistake in editorial policy—nor do the newspapers anywhere tell you the one fact which really matters. One reads nowhere There Was Once a Princess."

"Bah!" said the black dog.

"None the less, black dog, there was once a princess. It does not matter that I cannot quite recall my dealings with her. There was once a princess, and she yet lives, just around, as it were, the corner of my consciousness. Some day she will again become apparent. Meanwhile I cherish the knowledge that, somehow, she is not far from me, even now. All beauty speaks of her yet superior beauty; the west wind has a rumor of her; the pallid moon remembers my princess with envy; and every pleasure which one gets out of living is, in some way, a parable, and a promise also, of her returning."

"Which means," said the black dog, "that to be a more or less talked-about novel-writer, but an in-creasingly less talked-about novel-writer, does not content Smirt."

"To the contrary, black dog, life is wholly pleasant. All passes smoothly, equably. Admirers are sometimes a nuisance, but even that, in a way, is flattering. The books are made, and a competent prose style appears established in American letters. The quest is finished, in brief, with some handsomeness; and one rests contentedly after the achievement."

"But for no long while, Smirt. By-and-by, as you well know, these honors and these solid-seeming benefits must be put aside, and left casually behind, when you set forth on another quest, whose nature is not yet revealed to you."

"Oh, yes, black dog, that knowledge also lives on in, as one might say, the suburbs of consciousness. Meanwhile this staid breathing space, wherein one is a moderately successful artist, seems, I repeat, wholly pleasant."

"What, every hour of it, Smirt?"

"Every hour, black dog."

"Ah, but not every half-hour."

"In fact, black dog, I except perforce that half-hour about which you are talking."

THREE

*   *

LYING AWAKE

*

Indeed that odd half-hour was a trouble to him. There was no evading it. Each night he would sleep tranquilly and normally enough, for just six hours and a half. Then he wakened, always, and then, always, it would be a half-hour before he could again go back to sleep. It seemed a slight matter when one spoke of it by daylight to one's friends, one's wife, or, tentatively, to one's physician. It seemed by daylight a trifle.

Even when he first wakened, with that odd pang of terror and of inexplicable remorse, his reason told him that nothing frightful impended. Nothing frightful had happened, either, it was likewise the enforced part of his reason to assure him, in that first instant of waking. For he wakened in a panic remorse, without at all knowing what he was remorseful about. That was droll, his reason told him affably. When you regarded that rationally, it was amusing. Nor did

11

anything frightful await him, not even anything unpleasant. He was about to lie awake for a few minutes,
say, for a half-hour, at ease, in his comfortable bed.
Millions of his fellow creatures would be eager to exchange lots with him.

At this very instant, reason would point out, how
many persons must make shift to sleep upon park
benches or in flop houses, whatever flop houses happen to be. A great many people are dying at this very
instant; and nobody ever seems really to enjoy dying,
if you watch them closely. There is a flavor of some
disagreeable surprise and of a peevishness, even in the
most peaceful cases.

Think, reason exhorted, of how many thousands
of people are lying awake, at this very instant, in one
or another active sort of pain. What if you had back
that abscess of the inner ear? or if your teeth were
hurting again? What about appendicitis? You may
have an attack of it, at any moment, without the least
warning.

Remember, reason continued, that on the Thames
Embankment, and under Waterloo Bridge, the best
traditions of standard English fiction are being preserved, at this very instant, by quite a number of social outcasts. "So 'elp me, guv'nor," they mutter, as
they toss restlessly upon cold and damp, hard flag-
stones. Of course it is several hours earlier in Eng-

land, so that they are all up and about, long ago; but the principle is the same. One should always be guided by principle.

And you, you are entirely comfortable here in bed, not even a crumpled rose leaf, like the what-was-his-name, observed reason drowsily, where tired nature's sweet restorer knits up the ravelled sleave of something or other, not a sleeve as in coat, for the Temple edition has a note on it, but you have forgotten it, and what the dickens is the use of such notes, all segregated, and in such tiny type too, in the remote back of the book, when nobody gives Dickens the credit for inventing the stream of consciousness method, as begun by Jingle, and brought to perfection by Flora I-forget-who, in *Little Dorrit*, but it is a poor art that never re-Joyces nowadays, like Agathon running on like a rivulet of oil, so flow gently, sweet Afton, but how do they stay awake when they are writing it, for I am almost, almost asleep now, not as in Afton, Virginia, because that is a mountain, so do not make them out of mole-hills, but go right back to sleep like a good boy now, my precious lamb.

And again, thus wavering on the dear threshold of sleep, he was bludgeoned by anguish. He remembered that his childhood's nurse, she who had used so tenderly to urge him, as a precious lamb, to go right back to sleep like a good boy, had been dead now for many years; and to remember that, thrilled him with terror and with remorse. There were no grounds known to him for this remorse, nor was his terror in any way explainable. It was merely that these emotions, like tyrannizing giants, had dragged him back into panic wakefulness.

And with that, a shadowy crowd of persons once his intimates, and now dead, seemed gradually to approach him, with a certain air of reproval which stayed unexplained, these coming not quite into his thoughts, but, like the princess and like his knowledge of that unfulfilled quest, into, as it were, the suburbs of his consciousness, now that reason was asleep. It troubled one very intolerably to recollect by what trivial matters these persons had been engaged in the put-by time of their living, to recollect how unimportant and how irrevocably ended were all the doings of these dear dead: for into a great many lives, now done with, now dead as Hector or Hannibal, one had entered intimately, and had thus seen what concerns did actually engross the few years, the hours, or, better still, the seconds, in which men and women lived.

There was one instant, then another instant, then yet another, but only one instant at a time. You lived only in the instant which was present: that was a thought which, through no sound reason, seemed terrible. For no man had, at any time in his life, more than one instant of existence. Every man's past was fixed and removed from his control; his future was unfixed, but stayed equally uncontrollable. You had meanwhile your one instant of existence, your one clock-tick. . .Yes, life went by you with an inconceivable rapidity, with the rapidity of the small ribbon of film in a moving-picture machine. The screen (that would be his brain, he supposed) showed at each instant a different picture, if but slightly different, but always just one complete picture at one time: then the revealed picture disappeared forever: so did the trivial, the dull, the magnanimous, the prurient, or the merely comfortable instants of living flicker by you. You could not change or stop the ever escaping pictures, those highly complex pictures which had in them, not only color and sound, but smell and feeling and taste also.

That was nonsense, he remembered, as he turned over on the left side, finding a cool place on the pillow: you could not photograph a smell, nor did pictures have feeling and taste in them, either, except in quite another sense. All of it, however, seemed to be nonsense. All of it, all human life, appeared utterly inconsequent. . .Yet he enjoyed it, this flickering series of instants, which promised him, somehow, that by-

and-by a forthcoming instant would reveal a loveliness, a complete satisfaction, which did not as yet exist.
It was this which kept life always interesting, this im-
plied and perhaps untruthful promise of a beauty and
of a happiness which did not as yet exist, but to which,
by-and-by, he would be attaining.

For he knew that his own life was different in nature from the lives of his temporary associates. They
passed, fritteringly; but he was not thus transient.
Even if, as that confounded black dog had said, he had
not yet found his suitable audience, his books endured, to delight the cultured and the urbane everywhere, and to delight oncoming ages also. And besides that, he himself endured, with a fixed purpose,
which he would presently discover. His living had its
determined and lofty goal, if only one could recollect
just what it was.

To the other side (and suiting action to thought,
he now turned over again) he had once dreamed,
more or less like the philosopher Chuang Tzu, that
he was a blue-bottle fly; and the resultant problem
had never been straightened out quite satisfactorily
...To the other side, even though he did not really
desire to have absolutely everybody talking about him
at every moment (as that irrational black dog had
suggested) , and even though "an acute but honorable
minority of readers" contented any reasonable sort of

writer as an audience, yet he did remain unknown to the public at large. . .

He jumped now, a little, as he put aside these disturbing reflections. Yes, that wakeful half-hour, in the time before dawn, was troublesome, but there was no need to bother about it on this pleasant afternoon. It was better to continue conscientiously upon one of those therapeutic walks which the family physician recommends, with an affable obstinacy, after you have reached the angina age. It was gratifying, too, to observe that as you passed among your fellow townsmen, in the cool of this pleasant evening, the public at large were all speaking, with appropriate interest and with a hitherto unnoted deference, as to the main glory of Richmond-in-Virginia. It showed that the black dog did not know what he was talking about.

FOUR

* *

"THY NEIGHBOR AS THYSELF"

*

That is Smirt, the very great author," an intelligent looking baker remarked to his companions—"yonder tall and dark and superbly handsome gentleman."

"He is more beautiful than a Greek god," declared the butcher, who was plainly a well-read person. "I would describe his appearance as Praxitelean."

"But how unimportant, my friends, is his virile comeliness in comparison with his other gifts!" cried the candlestick maker.

"Born of an old and distinguished family, with an authentic coat of arms," said Tom, "the genius of Smirt has promoted him to opulence and fame alike."

"The books of Smirt," Dick commented, "are read with deference and a complete lack of understanding, all over the world, in every language. I have seen his picture in two newspapers."

Then Harry said, a little enviously: "His morals

18

are by no means what they should be, and all women pursue him. He has dug much in other men's ditches."

"In its every passage his life," declared Madame Quelquechose, "has been an incredible romance, for Smirt has indulged every passion with discrimination; he burns always with the required gem-like flame, and he has philosophically sampled its every scorching. There is no emotion which has not been tested and described handsomely by Smirt."

"Indeed I have it upon the very best authority," said Señora Etcetera, "that forgery, arson, rape, barratry, plagiarism, driving while under the influence of intoxicants, manslaughter, piracy on the high seas, false income tax returns, and offences against the person, against property (either with or without violence) and offences against the currency also—I have heard, I repeat, that such matters are the daily diversion of Smirt."

"That is as it should be," stated Lady Ampersand, "for these naughty doings enrich the mind, and they broaden the point of view of a writer, besides adding to the interest of his biography."

"The biography of Smirt, my friends," said Anon, "will never be printed in anything like a complete state. The fact is well known that he has his dinner jackets tailored with two outside pockets so as to keep contraceptives always handy; and his own relatives admit he has done everything which makes a person sophisticated. These matters are familiar to all Richmond-in-Virginia."

"You need add no more," remarked Ibid, "for, as a writer who am myself pretty widely quoted, I know that such enormities cannot be mentioned in any biography intended for school and college use. Yet genius creates its own laws."

"You may well say that," the world and his wife agreed comfortably. "There is really nothing like genius."

"I think his books are perfectly wonderful," declared Mrs. Murgatroyd; "and whenever I see Smirt I simply cannot imagine what it was I saw in Murgatroyd."

*   *

FIVE

RATIONALITY INTERVENES

*

Now the provoker of all this adulation was not listening any longer to the public at large. Instead he was
wondering why these persons, who in every other respect spoke with tact, courtesy, intelligence, and discrimination, should all be emulating that uncivil
black dog by calling him Smirt, when the fact stayed
almost certain his name was not Smirt. It seemed an
odd thing, too, that for the moment he could not recall his real name; but he had not any doubt this
name would come back to him by-and-by.

"Meanwhile let us respect public opinion," he exhorted himself. "These persons can see in me but
Smirt, a supreme genius who is in every way superb
and enviable. With what inadequacy do they comprehend me! The truth as to this being whom they
erroneously call Smirt is far more great and more profound and more strange, I now perceive. It is unde-
niable that this truth eludes me for the present. I

perceive its existence, but I do not grasp its connection with anything else. Yet this truth relates, I know, to an eternal questing which is not yet finished. Since I cannot well be the Wandering Jew, who was circumcised, it would seem to follow in plain logic that Ahasuerus may have his complement in the Errant Christian. To put the matter even more precisely, I am no doubt the Peripatetic Episcopalian."

For an urbane person, he reflected, must naturally be an Episcopalian, taking his beliefs not too seriously, as luxuries rather than as necessities. Between piety and atheism, then, the Peripatetic Episcopalian would go his discreet way, admiring the fervors of both now and again, but admiring them, as one does the flowers in a public park, without touching either. To believe, absolutely and indissuadably, as did such quaint persons as Methodists and Free-thinkers, that you yourself knew the truth as to religion, or as to anything else, must always be for the Peripatetic Episcopalian an unattainable naïveté. At odd times you might almost desire such naïveté.

Meanwhile the Peripatetic Episcopalian had his unrivalled Book of Common Prayer, he had his one safe religious tenet, that Thomas Cranmer wrote excellent prose. Apart from that dogma he was well content (in so far as Smirt could recall what Pater had written about Botticelli) "to accept that middle world in

which men take no side in great conflicts, and decide
no great causes, and make great refusals; setting thus
for himself the limits within which art, undisturbed
by any moral ambition, does its most sincere and
surest work."

Afterward Smirt said: "On the other hand, I once
dreamed, more or less like the philosopher Chuang
Tzu, that I was a blue-bottle fly. I was then conscious
only of my thoughts, my interests, and my beliefs as
a blue-bottle fly, and unconscious of my present individuality as a man. I awoke from that dream, and it
seemed to me I was myself again. Still, I cannot be
certain. Still, I do not know whether I was at that
time a gifted literary genius dreaming I was a blue-
bottle fly, or whether I am at this time a blue-bottle
fly dreaming I am a literary genius."

It was not, he reflected, that any urbane and literate
person could object to being a fly. To the contrary,
Homer had lauded the fly, finding no higher praise
possible for any warrior than to liken his boldness in
battle to the boldness, during the dog days, of a fly,
which although driven away once and again from the
skin of men, still is eager to bite, and sweet to it is the
blood of mankind.

And Lucian also, Lucian had devoted an entire
essay to praising the beauty and wisdom and musical
gifts, and yet other virtues, of the fly, an essay in which

Lucian had laid special emphasis upon the fact, not very generally known even to-day, that if a little ashes be sprinkled on a dead fly, it experiences a second birth, and stands up, spreading its delicate and peacock-hued wings for a fresh start in life,—a circumstance, as Lucian conceded half-enviously, which could not but be interpreted as a proof that the soul of every fly is both rational and immortal, where the soul of man may well be made of less durable stuff, inasmuch as the soul of a fly, after returning somehow from an insectean Hades, can thus recognize and reanimate its discarded body.

You could not desire better sponsors. No living literary genius had ever been commended by both Homer and Lucian, no mere man of letters could now hope to be mentioned thus honorably by these masters. . .And yet, after all, one's flyship was but a possibility. It might be a deluding mirage. To imagine that you were born of the Calliphora family, and related closely to all the Muscoidea and kin to the great race of Diptera, might even be an excursion into that overweening and highly dangerous pride termed *hubris*; for after weighing every bit of the evidence, you had no sound legal proof with which to establish in any court of law that Smirt was a bluebottle fly who was now dreaming about you.

For this reason Smirt said also: "The problem baffles me. It is plain that I move in a dream. Yet in no way known to me can I deduce from a dream the person who is dreaming it. He is Smirt, obviously. Ah, but who is Smirt? As to that profound question I remain unassured. He may very well be a blue-bottle fly, most nobly descended from the Diptera, through the Calliphora family; but with equal likelihood he may be the Peripatetic Episcopalian, a personage no less splendid. I do not know. I know only that in this dream, no matter who may happen to be dreaming it, my desire reaches beyond the doings and the rewards of an applauded literary genius, about whom all the public at large are now talking. And the moral of that is (as the dear Duchess put it) that I must satisfy this desire, the very instant I have discovered its nature."

"Perhaps, Smirt, it is your desire to give a brief interview to the *Times-Leader*," the young man suggested.

*   *

SIX

REASONS FOR NOT TALKING

*

No," Smirt replied, "it is not my desire to 'give' either a brief interview or a lengthy interview for the *Times-Leader* in this place. I cannot reasonably be expected to display my wit, my erudition, my profundity, or in fact any of my talents, upon a street corner."

"Yet your publisher suggested, sir—"

"That is possible. With time, with sore travail, does each author learn that the ways of every known publisher resemble the axiomatic peace of God."

"And so—" said the young man.

"Nevertheless," Smirt explained, "I really cannot talk with you just now."

"But—" said the young man.

"To the other side," Smirt went on, "since I can think of no civil pretext for avoiding the intrusion, I must assure you, my dear sir, that should you call at my home about four o'clock to-morrow afternoon,

your advent will be to me a source of considerable
pleasure; and that with unbounded delight I will
then 'give' the newspaper interview for which you
have misguidedly asked. The affair is thus settled.
And yet it really does seem rather an unexhilarating
manner of wasting our time."

I am sure of this fact (Smirt continued, in the while
that he went on to explain why Smirt could not talk
to the representative of the *Times-Leader*) because,
under varying surnames, and wearing slightly different very young faces, you have called on me aforetime,
very, very often, at the bidding of one or another of
the local papers. Your questions, during the last
twenty-five years, have varied in their objectives, but
never in their depth and seriousness and futility. Nor
indeed have they varied widely. Not ever, for example, during the last twenty-five years, has any representative of the Virginian press failed to inquire,
"What will be the future trend of literature in the
South?" and, "Whom do you consider to have the
most promising future among our younger Southern
writers?" I am forlornly convinced therefore that, at
not later than two minutes after four o'clock to-morrow afternoon, you also, my dear sir, will have asked
me both these questions, quite gravely.

Not at all (Smirt resumed) will your polite summons to unveil the future perturb me. I shall face both queries, I can assure you, without replying "Alackaday!" or *"Misserime!"* or even *"Ototoi!"* For whensoever anybody, in any walk of life, is "interviewed," then as a matter of course he is called on to prophesy. It is possible to unfold no morning paper without facing a half-column instance or so of magnates vaticinating as to next month's stock market and the next quarter's upswing, or of tourists just off the gangplank who are reassuringly conversant with Europe's future (specialising at this present moment in the destinies of Russia and of Germany), or of realtors lyric over the impendent boom in real estate. And what publicist anywhere (save only, perhaps, Mr. Roosevelt) remains ignorant as to what the President intends to do next? It seems but fair that in this welter of omniscience the most obtuse of writers should know all about the future of literature in the South.

So I shall not reply to these perennial questions truthfully, "I don't know." To admit any such nescience would be humiliating beyond human endurance so long as at least a dozen persons continue to subscribe tó the *New Republic,* and thus find all future happenings made plain as an equal number of pikestaves. I dislike appearing unique in my ignorance. I prefer to hedge; I elect to answer all "interviewers" with a civil pretence of taking them seriously; and therefore, at two minutes after four o'clock to-morrow afternoon, I shall attempt to disguise, in resonant and shifty babblings, modeled after the general style of the New York *Times'* editorial page, my lack of any firm interest in literary trends or in any of our younger Southern writers.

It is not that even in my most private thoughts I disparage these matters. I mean only that, if any author dared venture into printed frankness, I would have to say to you, necessarily, that it was my appointed task to construct my own books in the way which seemed best to me. I was thus forced (I would continue) throughout the passing away of many highly enjoyable years, to run counter to all current literary trends, and to disregard them. You question me (I would point out) as to a subject with which I have cultivated—resolutely, throughout my whole life as an author—all possible unacquaintance. Inasmuch as I have never taken holy orders, I do not believe that complete ignorance of the topic in hand can peculiarly qualify me to dispose of it with authority.

Even so, I prefer to be fair. I remark that, perhaps throughout the entire South, but most certainly in the State of Virginia, the liberal arts now flourish to an unprecedented extent. Mr. Charles Gilpin, the noted actor who but lately created the title rôle of *The Emperor Jones*, I would remind you, was a native born Virginian. So, I believe, was Miss Peggy Hopkins Joyce, whose cognate genius for acting is attested by the number of her husbands. And Mr. Bill Robinson, the famous tap dancer, is yet another jewel—as one should say, a black diamond—in the cultural diadem of Virginia.

In still another field of æsthetics may Virginia point with maternal pride to that gifted cantatrice, Miss Kate Smith, whose voice makes melody in the homes of a vast radio audience thrice a week, proclaiming the merits of I forget whose cigars. And in what state, I demand of the welkin, was reared and nurtured Mr. Freeman Gosden, that pre-eminent expositor of Pepsodent's never-ending *comédie humaine*? Echo answers, I admit, "Maine." But her answer is not true. The world knows that Mr. Gosden likewise is a native born Virginian.

Do not think me a mere boaster, in the best Southern tradition. It is needful for a Virginian thus to catalogue at the top of his voice these finer flowers of our present-day cultural renaissance. And my point is not merely that all these Virginian artists prospered through the simple and unarduous recipe of leaving Virginia. What seems to me far more important, and more instructive, and more full of promise as con-

cerns the future, is the attested fact that Virginia
nowadays honors her leading artists liberally. Did
Charles, the great emperor, stoop to pick up the brush
of Titian? With a celerity no less imperial or gleaming, so often as Miss Kate Smith delights Virginia
with a visit, does the Governor of Virginia, attended
by his gold-braided staff, arise very early in the morning to meet her Pullman with plenary homage. And
when Mr. Robinson frequents Richmond-in-Virginia,
then even in the lobby of our most fashionable hotel
is Mr. Bill Robinson to be seen dancing nimbly with
this or the other fair Caucasian maiden, his pupil,
amid the respectful applause of our city's élite, so
properly have we learned to esteem the art of Mr.
Robinson as weighed against yesterday's inter-racial
taboos.

Concerning the enthusiasm with which Virginia
greets the most widely known of her children, Mr.
Gosden, I can but remark that it staggers belief and
checks traffic in the public highways. It does not seem
enough that *en grande tenue* the citizens of Richmond have conferred upon this all-conqueror the
appropriate gift of a sword. The pomps of that chiv-
alrous ceremony did but feebly indicate our fond
and inexpressible pride in the most famous of living
Virginians. Everywhither do such throngs attend the
passing of our supreme artist that when, with his con-

frère in comedy, Mr. Charles Correll, he last entered a Richmond bank, it was found needful to put a placard in the front window explaining that no "run" on the establishment was in progress, but that "Amos 'n' Andy" were inside. We Virginians have taken, in short, the main step toward autochthonous art: we have evolved, we have learned to revere, our own æsthetic.

With the cultural ideals of the South in a condition thus thriving, I do not doubt that, in the former Confederacy, literature will begin, by-and-by, to share with her sister arts in public esteem. This very afternoon I have overheard remarks from the butcher, the baker, and the candlestick maker which displayed a praiseworthy interest in polite letters. That fact is encouraging. It induces me to look forward to a time when every Southern household of the better class will contain its book as well as its electric refrigerator; when painters and musicians will be regarded in the South almost as seriously as aldermen; when its statuary will serve needs not wholly canine; and when Southerners will accord, in brief, to the career of every kind of creative artist a quota of condonation.

My point is merely that the dawn of this approvable day (despite the highly encouraging symptoms noted this afternoon) is not quite as yet apparent. And so I admit that, to my finding, for any young Southerner to commence author, just at present, does show such disregard for the opinions of his more mature and better-thought-of neighbors as (even before I have looked over his book and decided that, after all, I do not have to read it) does prejudice me as to his mental balance. One who forfeits thus wantonly the respect of his daily associates, and of his abashed family, is not, I reflect, the exact person with whom the judicious would foregather, even in print. So I do, it may be, avoid the books of our younger Southern authors somewhat more expeditiously than I shy away from the newest balderdash by oncoming American authors spawned in some other section of the Republic. I do it unconsciously, because of my respect for the common-sense standards of my own better-thought-of neighbors.

I shall say no one of these things to-morrow afternoon, although I believe you would sympathize did I become thus loquacious. As behooves a normally intelligent and well-reared young Southerner, you also are no whit interested in such flimsy makeshifts for personal rapture, and for personal experience, and for personal notions, as literature keeps in stock. You prefer these substitutes at a higher voltage in the moving pictures. You have been sent me-ward, by an irrational city editor, to get a "story" out of our talk to-morrow afternoon, a "story" which will appear unobtrusively, some four days later, interning my alleged "philosophy of life," with my portrait, very far inside the paper, between the quips of the local humorist and the day's special bargains at the cut-rate drugstore. And I am abetting you because of my publisher's firm belief that such not-ever-read reading-matter makes valuable "publicity" which will enable him (so lively is the Baptist faith) to sell books in remunerative quantities on the south side of the Potomac.

The impending "interview," in brief, must be for both of us a nuisance to be endured restively. We two are the victims of circumstance. None can help us. Nobody will help us. We can but try to make our shared boredom as lenient as may prove possible, with the aid of a few *hors-d'œuvres*, and of Ravished Virgin cocktails, and of much continuous cigarette smoking, in the while we discuss the future trend of Southern literature, and which one of our younger Southern writers has the most promising future, in the North.

All these things (Smirt concluded) we will do resignedly to-morrow afternoon. My point is merely that to-day happens not to be to-morrow. To-day I happen to be rather busy in the middle of a dream, quite apart from the circumstance that in this dream

REASONS FOR NOT TALKING

I am standing on a street corner. To-day, in brief, I really cannot talk with you upon any subject whatever. I have, you conceive, a previous engagement with the young woman who is now peeping at me from out of this gateway, although I do not desire her, either, I am afraid. . .

SEVEN

*　　*

A LOST LEGEND

*

The girl was wistful and young, and she was well enough to look at, in an unimportant dark fashion. She had youth and health, which are fine possessions, to be sure, but even so, are not remarkably rare. No, Smirt did not desire this girl; yet he could almost, although not wholly, remember her.

She might perhaps be one of those not quite grasped memories which troubled him in the dawn, when he lay abed, not exactly awake and yet far from sleeping. He could very nearly recall that this girl's unimportant young face had passed restively through his dreams in one or another of those lonely dawns, just as he almost knew what doom it was that had touched this girl, darkly and ruthlessly, in a legend which he did not at this instant remember.

He had it, though, in part; she was the Princess Who Spins; and because of her spinning she had been thrust out of the magical lands behind this cobweb-covered gate, to wander about in common daylight, homeless and unremembered. He pitied this young girl in her exile; he liked her appearance: but Smirt desired other matters, and he was in fair hope to find out by-and-by what these matters might be. So he said only,—

"A good day to you, Arachne."

"A good day to you, Smirt."

"Ah, ah! And why do you also think my name to be Smirt?"

"But in a dream one always knows the names of people."

"That is true, Arachne. And since you are an exile from legend, and legends are closely akin to dreams, I do not doubt you are right. It may be that in this odd dream of mine I am indeed Smirt, and that Smirt is a blue-bottle fly. I can perceive no least evidence to the contrary. And for what, Arachne, are you looking in this irrational dream?"

She answered: "Men have forgotten my legend. The enraged goddess, the Gray-Eyed-One, decreed that every man who looked me full in the face should forthwith forget my legend. And I too have forgotten my legend, every ancient word of it, all except the long doom which was put upon me. But at times the sorrow and the faded colors and the stiff strangeness of my legend trouble me, from very far away, with a thin vexingness."

"To me also, Arachne," said Smirt, a little puzzled, "it seems that only an instant ago I knew your legend."

"But since then, Smirt, you have looked me full in the face."

"It is true. And that agreeable action explains, perhaps, this slight touch of aphasia. Yet your legend remains, as it were, just around the corner of my consciousness. Whether in that legend you were really a princess, or only her jealous elder sister, or a depraved sorceress, or a shepherdess, or it may be a dryad, there is no logical way of telling; but an illogical whisper tells me you are the Princess Who Spins."

The girl looked about her cautiously. She said, with confiding frankness:

"That whisper whispers the truth, Smirt. The trouble is, that I too have forgotten my legend. I recall only that the enraged goddess struck me with a shuttle. That was her way of condemning me to spin in an eternal exile from the legend which I have forgotten."

"Yet you do not spin, I imagine, like a top—or like a dervish?"

This widened by a great deal the rather pretty

brown eyes of Arachne. But she said only, after a moment's hesitation,—

"No, Smirt, I spin, as becomes a good housewife, on a spinning-wheel."

"And for what thing, I repeat, except it may be a spinning-wheel, can you, who are an exile from legend, be seeking here in this cobweb-covered gate?"

"I am looking, Smirt, as every well-conducted girl must do, for a husband to provide me with a home in which I may do my spinning."

"Ah, but I," Smirt explained, "am already married. And Jane, I am certain, would not approve of bigamy. Her principles are beyond reproach."

"Nor do I want half a husband either, Smirt, but a whole husband. So my principles are as good as hers."

"Yet one should take things in order, Arachne. It is excellent for every woman to have a husband; but he should come to you in due state, after a lover or two has ridden before him as his heralds."

The girl's dark little face appeared even darker now under the shadow of discontent. She remarked resignedly:

"He will be my lover, just at first. It is a thing all women have to put up with. But men get sensible by-and-by."

"They get older, my dear."

39

"To begin with, I am not your dear, and in the second place, whether they get older or more sensible, it comes to the same thing."

"I apologize, Arachne, and I desire, with all possible respect, to know what it does come to."

"It comes, Smirt, to that never-ending spinning and that weaving and that embroidery, and to all the other things which I want to be doing."

But such notions did not delight Smirt. He said gravely:

"These petty avocations are not suited to a person of your high origin, Arachne, in an old legend. You turn from romance to realism; and to do that is unworthy. For one ought to cherish such beautiful nonsense, Arachne, and to keep faith steadfastly with all those impossible things which are not true, but which ought to be true."

Now the girl shook her head, replying: "I had a palace, once, or at least I think that I once had a palace, very long ago when Idmon reigned as a great prince in Lybia. To-day I desire only a home in which I may rule fondly. We will need also a small shop, to keep us going, and a few babies. Perhaps two boys and a girl would be better, just to start with."

"You have then," Smirt inquired, "some marked out and, as the world averages, some fairly lucky man in mind?"

"Him!" she remarked, with disfavor. "No, I try not to think about him any more than I have to. Still, there does have to be a man to help me get the babies; and besides that, somebody will have to tend the shop."

Smirt nodded affably.

"I can perceive at least your point of view, Arachne. I can tender you, at any rate, my compliments on your directness. Whatever you were yesterday, to-day you have become what is called a domestic woman; and I wonder if you have been husband hunting in yonder?"

"You talk nonsense, Smirt, for it is well known there is no marriage or giving in marriage in that place behind me."

"You speak rather strangely, my dear—"

"To begin with—"

And at that, Smirt spread out both his hands, gaily remorseful.

"I know. I apologize again, Arachne, and I remark only that I never saw a gateway so thick with cobwebs as is this gateway. It is more like the lair of a spider than it is like a gateway. Oh, but yes, beyond any doubt, Arachne, this is a strange gate through which you have walked into my dream."

"It very well may be, Smirt, for it leads to a strange place."

"And what is that place called, Arachne?"

She told him.

"Oh, but come now," Smirt replied, laughing, "that is an irrational and an excessive name for any person to be giving his home in this select residential section. Yet I have noticed that the retired business man is given to these outbursts of wild fancy."

"He is not retired from business," the girl said,— "as yet."

"And how is this unretiring person called?"

She told him that also.

Smirt took her astonishing meaning. "You tell me that beyond this very wall He is to be found! Oh, but come now, this must be seen to. I am grateful to you. And do not bother, my dear child, about your lost legend. You shall be restored in due course to all its glories, to its fine improbabilities, and to its bereaved inhabitants, who, I am sure, must miss you a great deal. Goddess or no goddess, it is not fitting that an unchaperoned young woman who began life as a mythical figure should be condemned to live at loose ends in the queer world which the newspapers tell about. I shall see to that likewise."

She reached up, touching his shoulder, and coming much nearer to him.

"But, Smirt,—you speak now of the impossible."

"The most of my doings, Arachne, are impossible.

42

I have often noticed it. My wife also refers to the fact, now and then, when something has occurred to upset her."

"And besides," Arachne declared, "with that Jane of yours, who I am sure must watch you like a hawk, and probably has every reason to, what with the way you rattle on without giving the girl a chance to get in a word edgewise, and besides, even if I did rather like you, we do not really know each other as yet, Smirt, and it is not right for us to be together in this lonesome place, where there is no telling what impudence you might be up to, now it is growing darker and darker, with no one in sight of us, so that I would not be able to get any help, no matter how loudly I might scream—"

"My dear young woman," Smirt interrupted crisply, "do stop fiddling with my coat button! and scat! I mean, merely as a beguiling ingénue, in which rôle you are an agreeable commonplace. As an exile from romance, do you by all means remain here, at your proper distance, and accept my sworn oath to restore you to your lost estate in the lands beyond common-sense."

"I am grieved that you should have quite misunderstood me, Smirt, for I am not in the least that kind of girl; and I wonder whatever oath you are talking about?"

"I am talking about that oath, Arachne, which I now swear by such matters as I cordially reverence. I refer to the acumen of Sir Thomas Browne, which first perceived that fine prose should be kept undebased by deep thought; to the theology of William Congreve, through which the unpardonable sin was found to be clumsiness; and to the trimness of Robert Louis Stevenson, which completely baffles description. I refer to the painstaking and suave inclusiveness of Pater; to the higher carelessness of Saki; and to the pleasant eddies, to the ampleness, and to the ultimate, the ineffable rightness, of every paragraph which was written by W. M. Thackeray. I refer also to the general contents of my own works. It is by these seven great mysteries that I now give you my oath, Arachne, to restore to you your lost estate in the lands beyond common-sense. In the mean while, you have told me that beyond this wall He is to be found in person; and as a Peripatetic Episcopalian, I esteem it my plain duty to investigate, first of all, your surprising report."

With that said, Smirt pushed open the cobweb-covered gate, and he went in to the All-Highest.

PART TWO

OVERLOOKING A UNIVERSE

* *

*

"He took a cymbal or bell, and rang there-with, as they use to ring to dinner in cloisters, at the sound whereof many creatures of divers kinds came down from the mount, some like apes, some like cats, some having faces like men, to the number of 4200 of these creatures, all crying out,—'Treason against the United States shall consist only in levying war against them, or in adhering to their enemies, giving them aid and comfort.' "

*　　*

EIGHT

THE ALL-HIGHEST CONFIDES

*

The All-Highest was a perturbed looking elderly gentleman, with a benevolent bald forehead and a superb white beard. It was slightly puzzling to observe that the All-Highest had two short horns, and that His right foot was like the hoof of a goat. It seemed odd also that in this place there should be nothing except opaque gray clouds, upon one of which the All-Highest was sitting, with a small book in His lap.

But Smirt had other matters to consider, now that, after accepting one of Smirt's cigarettes, the All-Highest was speaking of George Bernard Shaw with virtually American disfavor. "For I do frankly consider, Smirt, that in this rigmarole about a Black Girl, which I have just been looking over, Mr. Shaw has disparaged My Book in a most unfriendly manner."

"I would distinguish, All-Highest," replied Smirt,

leaning back comfortably upon his own cloud. "In the first place, the book—by which I do not mean Your Bible, but only *The Adventures of the Black Girl in Her Search for God*—has been out a great while. The cognoscenti have forgotten it very completely, for we do not regard gravely any book which antedates the present publishing season—"

"Yes, but all our books come to us, Smirt, through the Salvation Army. People do not give them any new books."

"—For in our larger centres of culture," Smirt continued, "books deteriorate rapidly. It is due, I am told, partly to the shallowness of modern culture and partly to the great amount of sulphur dioxide in the atmosphere of our cities, due to combustion—"

"Yes, but," said the All-Highest, "we were not talking about sulphur dioxide, and I do not see how we ever got on any such topic."

"In fact, All-Highest, it is my misfortune to have an over-vigorous and too inclusive mind," said Smirt, frankly. "My thoughts for this reason embrace a wide variety of subjects with a quickness which many persons before You, sir, have found some difficulty in following—"

"But we were not talking about your mind, Smirt."

"Now that You mention it, I believe You are right.

I was saying that in the second place, Mr. Shaw must be regarded as one of the larger suns in the astronomy of English literature."

"Oh, but were you saying that, Smirt?" the All-Highest asked, doubtfully,—"for it seems an odd thing I did not hear you."

"Yes," said Smirt, "one may no more deny the brilliancy of his genius than one may question the brightness of the sun."

Now the All-Highest clutched at His white hair with both hands and appeared slightly worried. "It was I who made the sun, Smirt. And it really is rather nice and shiny, I think; but I quite honestly do not see how we got to talking about the sun either, nor what it has to do with a most uncivil Irishman."

"I mean, All-Highest, that, after reading every word of the book now in Your hand, the thought occurred to me that upon at least two occasions the award of the Nobel Prize for Literature has been self justifying. I mean that after the 1930 award Mr. Sinclair Lewis responded in kind by giving to the Nobel Prize Fund an amount of invaluable advertising such as could not otherwise have been secured for double the money. I mean also that when the 1925 award was made to Mr. Bernard Shaw, as the author 'who had mostly contributed to the benefit of mankind during the preceding year,' the fact that Mr. Shaw had pub-

49

lished no book during the preceding year did cause a noticeable number of persons to interpret the seeming compliment as a rather brutally accurate criticism of his later writings."

The All-Highest brightened so visibly that Smirt perceived he was on the right track. And Smirt continued:

"For what, after all, do we find in the trumpery tale which has had the misfortune to displease You. A black girl sets forth to search for You, conveniently equipped with her Bible and a knobkerry—"

"Only this morning, Smirt, I looked that up in the dictionary. It seems that a knobkerry is the Kafir equivalent of a shillalah."

"Quite so, All-Highest. Well, and as I was saying, she encounters You in a number of Your avatars, as You appeared variously to Moses, to Job, to Koheleth, to Micah, and to Jesus. All these does the black girl confound, seriatim, with the logic of Voltaire and the knobkerry of Mr. Shaw. Under the combined assault each one of Your avatars vanishes: and then— for we face here a flash of wit designed to captivate the village atheist—then likewise vanishes yet another bit of the Bible."

The old gentleman's brow empurpled. He said:

"It is to that, to that infamous slander, I object in particular. So many persons have disproved My existence, from time to time, that I do not at all mind being regarded as an obsolete superstition. A great many of my best friends are atheists. But I do resent any such jealous reflections on the enduring qualities of My Book, which is still selling excellently."

"As a fellow author, All-Highest, I delight to recognize in You the auctorial temperament," said Smirt pensively. "As a fellow author I sympathize. I would but point out that after all these set-tos with You, sir, the black girl decides—yes, here it is, sir, at the bottom of page 74—'that it is wiser to take Voltaire's advice by cultivating her garden and bringing up her pickaninnies than to spend her life imagining she can find a complete explanation of the universe by laying about her with a knobkerry.' "

"And what, Smirt, do you infer from that?"

"I find in that sentence, All-Highest, something very like a formal palinode. It is a sentence which leads me to imagine that, after laying about him for some and forty years with his own knobkerry—with the shillalah of a peculiarly fine intelligence—at least one free-thinker did not ever light on 'a complete explanation' of any universe which was populated by both his admirers and Your admirers. I infer, in brief, from this sentence, that a free-thinker, think he never so freely, and for no matter how many decades, may come to notice that he does not know everything, not even at the comparative maturity of his later seventies, not even after some forty years of explaining everything with entire lucidity; and I believe that every free-thinker is called upon by-and-by to face—if but obliquely, if only for an instant—this surprising outcome."

The All-Highest smiled. He declared, in half-chuckling protest:

"Come now, Smirt, that appears a great deal to deduce from one sentence; yet there may be something in what you say. And with your permission I will try another one of those excellent cigarettes."

"In fact, sir," Smirt continued, "this is a state of mind which is reached sooner or later by the best informed. No one of us understands everything. I myself, for example, do not know what De Witt Clinton is thinking about so intently on this United States Internal Revenue cigarette stamp. I do not know why the clock on the front page of the *Herald Tribune* is set at twelve minutes after six; nor why the King of Hearts and the Jack of Clubs are the only male court cards not to have a mustache; nor why a barber's pole should always revolve its three-colored spiral downwards. What lightness, what élan, I have often reflected, sir, would be gained did this pole revolve more aspiringly upwards, with the appropriate optimism of its owner's imaginings in regard to the benefits of shampoos and of singeing and of hair tonics—"

"These are indeed deep mysteries, Smirt; but we were not talking about shampoos, nor do I perceive what hair tonics have to do with any jealous and silly attacks on My Book—which, I might mention, is still selling excellently."

"I was about to observe, All-Highest, that every at all rational free-thinker must come by-and-by to question the main article of his own faith, as it was defined by Mr. Gilbert Chesterton, in the remote days when Mr. Chesterton had genius, that because something has satisfied generations of men it must be untrue. With a little more experience, sir, one begins to suspect that not even God can be disposed of by having at Him with a knobkerry. Under such treatment God vanishes, it is true: but it seems equally true that God may, just possibly, not find in that special form of address any reason for taking the addresser into His complete confidence."

After glancing everywhither, from under His shaggy white brows, and after making sure nobody was listening, the All-Highest spoke, in a confidential lowered voice, saying,—

"I admit, simply between ourselves, Smirt, that I do not find assault and battery an endearing ritual of worship, howsoever popular it becomes nowadays."

"And I promise You, All-Highest," Smirt replied, reassuringly, "that I shall never approach You in this fashion. I confess to a little dubiety whensoever anybody takes the bleak trouble to point out that through no human logic can be justified Your existence, sir. It occurs to me, I mean, that before advancing this two-edged argument one would be called upon, first, to justify in logic one's own existence; and I have yet to meet the man who could do this."

"Come now," said the old gentleman, as pleased as in the cliché is Punch, "but that is handsomely said. You speak well, Smirt, with a broad-mindedness which I do not often encounter among modern writers. Such speaking deserves a reward. So to you, Smirt, I will gladly explain everything."

Thereupon the All-Highest explained everything. He explained first about barbers' poles, and about the King of Hearts (but without committing Himself, one way or the other, as to the Jack of Clubs), and about the *Herald-Tribune* clock, and about De Witt Clinton. Then the All-Highest went on to explain His conduct of the universe: and Smirt listened with ever-growing dismay.

"It does not please you, Smirt, to know that which no mortal man has known before you?"

"Oh, as to that, All-Highest, I appreciate Your confidence. I am honored, sir, I assure You. Nor is it quite my province, perhaps, to dictate to You in these cosmic affairs."

"Nevertheless, Smirt, do you speak your mind freely."

For an instant Smirt looked appraisingly at the gray cloudland which spread everywhither about them. All seemed most satisfactorily chaotic; and yet, as Smirt now knew, there was no chaos anywhere. It was a defect over which Smirt perforce shook his head. Thereafter Smirt answered, with urbane self-restraint:

"I can but say, sir, that Your methods are out-of-date. The entire system is an anachronism. And what is even more serious, it conflicts with the canons of civilized art."

"I had feared," the All-Highest replied, in an apologetic way, "that my methods could hardly hope for your approval. I have read your books, of course, with vast admiration and some unavoidable envy. You and I, Smirt, are creative artists who belong to different schools. You should allow for that fact before dismissing My work as of no merit at all."

"But this work of Yours, All-Highest, as You have confessed to me, is government. It has a formal plan. It is rational. It involves the long ago exploded notion of a Personal Creator. All these circumstances have been revealed to me rather over suddenly; and

I will not deny that the shock to my feelings is considerable. Little did I think, sir, in the long while that I was a communicant of the Protestant Episcopal Church, and worshipped You every Sunday morning, that You actually did exist; and far less did I suspect what You were up to. Your conduct during quite a number of centuries, I to-day perceive, has robbed human life of all lack of meaning. Your conduct of the universe, in brief, has amounted to a direct attack upon civilized art, in that You have left no target for irony. Yet what, I ask of You, what is to become of civilized art if all human life is not in truth a meaningless muddle which the artist observes with amused superiority?"

"Truly, Smirt," the All-Highest replied, blushing, "I had not thought of that point. When I began My work there were no civilized persons by whose advice I might profit, and so I had to arrange matters more or less in the light of My own judgment. And you really ought to allow me credit for having done the very best I could."

Smirt gave over a moment to profound meditation. He said then:

"All-Highest, I must be frank with You. To disparage the work of any person to his face is a thankless task. I would prefer to avoid any such seeming brutality: but the present situation is grave. And besides that, mind You, I do find Your universe to be full of many quite charming bits. Your sunsets, for example, Your kangaroos, Your Gila monsters, Your Presidents of the United States, and many of Your thunderstorms, show that You have real imagination, in Your own grotesque vein."

"Come now, but that is generous of you, Smirt. Commendation from Sir Hubert Stanley, you know, is praise indeed—"

"At character drawing, I admit," Smirt went on regretfully, "You do not excel. Your men and women are not always convincing, and suggest that You have never probed deeply into human nature. Yet nobody has a universal genius, and for such defects it would be hypercriticism to blame You."

"You really think, then, that with continued application, Smirt, I have a possible future?"

"Oh, yes, Your work displays promise, distinct promise! It is merely that You employ obsolete formulæ. So for Your own good, sir, I must tell You, in plain words, that this underlying coherent plan ruins everything. Your work, I now discover, has a formal plot: and plots, sir, plots were discarded long ago by the small civilized minority of authors."

"But what do you suggest, Smirt—?"

After an instant's reflection Smirt decided to apply the supreme test. He said,—

"It may be, All-Highest, that I can best illustrate my idea by relating a rather amusing story which occurs to me."

"Then do so, Smirt, for My sense of humor is remarkably keen."

"I hear and I obey, All-Highest. I obey the more readily because this droll anecdote concerns one of Your immediate servitors. I must tell You, then, that the next Bishop of Wyoming—"

"That the what, Smirt?"

"I apologize, sir. I had quite forgotten that all time is coincident to Your perception, since You are omnipresent. It is thus, of course, not possible for You to distinguish between the present bishop, the last bishop and the next bishop. But I do mean the next bishop. That is an essential point of the story."

"Very well then, Smirt. It sounds a little puzzling, I admit. . .However, you may go on."

"The next Bishop of Wyoming," Smirt resumed, "was famous for his partiality to scrambled eggs, a dish of which, through circumstances irrelevant to the story, he had never partaken. So well known was this foible that, upon a warm afternoon in May, a noted actress inquired of him, in a spirit of banter, 'Can you inform me, sir, what is the current rate of exchange?' With a twinkle in his eye, the bishop replied promptly, 'Madam, no wise man leads a horse to salt water.' The lady's confusion can be better imagined than described."

The All-Highest laughed heartily at this anecdote, and said:

"That is a woman, all over. Yes, Smirt, that is an uncommonly good story. Yes, yes, to be sure! And I only wish more of My bishops were as quick-witted."

At that, Smirt shook his head, and he sighed a little; but he said nothing.

"Nor do I deny," the All-Highest continued, "that I might have profited by forming Myself after superior models. We will let the future test that: and meanwhile, in evidence of my gratitude, I present you with this coin, for a lucky piece."

"I observe, All-Highest, that it is a forty reis coin issued in 1820 by John the Sixth, by the Grace of God, King of Portugal, Brazil and Algarvez. I duly admire his laurel wreath, so freely beribboned; his snub nose; and his three chins. But what shall I do with this coin?"

"Oh, you may do with it whatever you like, Smirt."

"I must do that in any case, sir, whether with or without a lucky piece."

"That appears likely. It is not utterly certain," replied the All-Highest, reflectively. "At all events, I would counsel you to preserve this coin, as a slight souvenir of our first meeting. And now, Smirt, as a fellow author, let us have your advice. I was thinking that in view of the gratifying success of My Book—which is still selling excellently,—I might do yet another book, Smirt. I mean something really mature, this time, and something a bit more up-to-date than the Bible, you understand. . ."

*   *

NINE

WHICH DEHORTS

*

Smirt said: "Come, let us raise for the All-Highest a lamentation. Begin, ye Muses, begin the funeral song: declare His folly unto the literati; make plain His blunders among the book clubs. With His right hand and His holy arm He would write yet another book."

Thereafter Smirt paused; and he shook his head in the while that, as became an American author, Smirt thought respectfully about the magnificos who in his country, at this time, reviewed current reading-matter. Smirt comprehended, only too well, how inadequate must seem the endowments and the creative powers of mere omnipotence when judged by Their standards. And furthermore, Smirt remembered what They invariably said about the next book by any author who had scored a popular hit with his first book.

For this reason Smirt continued: "Begin, ye Muses,

begin the funeral song; and narrate the curt epitaphs of the All-Highest in His second publishing venture. Between the Atlantic ocean and the Pacific ocean may His book hope to find no defender. 'It displays a sad falling off in inspiration,' will the Boston *Transcript* remark. The Hartford *Courant* will color its drooling unfavorably. A rumor speeding among the heathen, even into Staten Island and Brooklyn, will proclaim that Soskin hath not read the like of this bosh in ten years; yea, nor Kronenberger. In order to demolish this book will Granville Hicks yet again borrow the æsthetics, the writings, and the urbanity, of Upton Sinclair. In the *American Spectator* will appear the name of the All-Highest, unexplainedly, within mourning borders. Upon every Rural Free Delivery route, where the *New Yorker* delights the hired girl, even where the farmer's wife takes in *Vanity Fair*, and vice versa, will peasantry scoff at this book."

Afterward Smirt said: "Begin, ye Muses, begin the funeral song; for this book must die uncommended. Not even the facile fervors of William Lyon Phelps will acclaim this book surreptitiously, in his safe hiding place, between the covers of *Scribner's Magazine*. Gibes and a regal pitying, these only, must be the portion of this book. In Cincinnati Ted Robinson will smile upon this book with derision; nor will Fanny Butcher avert her dispraise in Chicago. The horoscope of this book will reveal the Kansas City *Star* as ill dignified, in the twelfth house, in the inimical House of Fishes. In Denver will Caroline Bancroft confess that the All-Highest fails to maintain His earlier promise. 'Nothing like so good as the Bible,' will be the blunt verdict of the *Portland Oregonian*. 'Now in its second large printing,' may the publishers of this book proclaim at utmost, speaking unveraciously."

Then yet again Smirt said: "Begin, ye Muses, begin the funeral song; for the South alone will remain silent and unscornful, not heeding this book, or any other book. All these testimonies have become for me a foreboding, and my counsellors likewise, now that I raise for the All-Highest a lamentation."

When he had ended his elegiac mingling of the Psalmist and Theocritus, Smirt remained silent—pondering, with a shared mind, upon the divine ways of book reviewers and upon the dilemma into which magnanimity had thrust him.

And Smirt said: "This really does need considering. Beyond doubt it is my duty, as a fellow church member, to dissuade the All-Highest from this crowning folly. To the other side, in this dream of mine—if it be a dream—I have promised to reinstate that little Arachne in her lost legend; and a gentleman must keep his word, whether he be awake or asleep."

It all appeared somewhat troubling. To find the All-Highest a rather obtuse and bemuddled person had been natural enough, since some such person was deducible by logic from all prior acquaintance with His handiwork—provided, of course, that you could manage to reconcile your religious faith as an Episcopalian with His actual existence. But to find Him endowed with the auctorial temperament was a discovery of a distinctly upsetting kind, because you knew that temperament only too well: no universe was safe in its keeping.

And to find Him on the point of publishing His second book, in an era so unfriendly to all which the naïve old gentleman represented, was a situation to perceive which had enkindled Smirt with a patronizing and tender, and yet fierce, protectiveness. He must shield this pathetic blunderer, he must without any delay preclude the All-Highest, from that cruel and silken derision which the All-Highest would incur, quite inevitably, by making any more revelations to mankind in the present state of American letters.

On the other hand, Smirt had given a plain promise to that little Arachne, to a female in distress. It was his duty to look after her lost estate without any delay. And chronologically at least, Arachne had the prior claim.

Yet Smirt was not twins. He could not simultaneously be in two places, upholding womanhood in one of these places, and protecting God in the other one of these places. It followed that the proper course for the Peripatetic Episcopalian, in these circumstances, required some calm thinking out.

*　　*

TEN

WHICH CONTINUES TO DEHORT

*

In the while that Smirt reasoned thus logically between the claims of his religious duties and the claims of his plighted faith, he saw that his admirers had pursued him. For now came running toward Smirt pell-mell the butcher, and the baker, and the candlestick maker, and Tom, and Dick, and Harry, and Madame Quelquechose, and Señora Etcetera, and Lady Ampersand, and the world and his wife, and Anon, and Ibid, and Mrs. Murgatroyd likewise.

All these cried out to the Peripatetic Episcopalian:

"Do not leave us, Smirt! We have a need of your nonsense. For hour by hour we must do that which hour by hour we did yesterday. We have many common-sense tasks to discharge: they fill up each day utterly; our reward is that we have food and sleep and our children and our portion of shallow laughter. We have our griefs also, but no deep griefs. The fixed round of our living prevents us from yielding up to any passion with our whole hearts. When love touches us, then must we yet think, with at least some part of our minds, about whether marriage would be quite sensible on our present income; about house rents; and whether it would be pleasant to have the beloved's family in and about the house forever? When death parts us from the most dear, then must we concern ourselves about a suitable plot in the cemetery, we must bargain with the mortician for the coffin. Also we must telephone to borrow black clothing, we must decide upon floral designs and pick out the pall bearers, and we must send in a notice to the newspapers, before we can find any time wherein to grieve for our dead."

They said then: "Do not leave us, Smirt! Our joys and our griefs are shallow: there is in our lives no dignity. But you, O Smirt, have skill to release us from many hundreds of small bonds. Your genius is as a delivering sword; of your wit and your fancy is made a shining pair of scissors. Snip, snip, they say, and then yet again, Snip. Thus are we set free from our packthread bondage; the many hundreds of small ties which confine us each in his proper station are clipped through. We become as the gods are, untrammeled. Our joys have majesty, our sorrows tread nobly, and beauty regards us with an unveiled face, very tenderly. We know then that our doom is less strong than we are. We forget our cousins and the family across the street and the first of the month and the tax collector and the unpaid dues at the country club. We observe only the many-colored and urbane world which Smirt has created for our delight, the land about which, like a superior Cook's guide, the fine art of Smirt leads us on a holiday outing."

And they said also: "Do not leave us, Smirt! We who are well-thought-of citizens must live drowsily without dreams. We can but borrow a dream here and there from the unpractical, and from the untruthful a friendly lie or two, to cheat us into warm magnanimity. Of your nonsense we have a grave need, to drug us into forgetfulness of our stupid selves and of our little manner of living. Our common-sense has confined us in a treadmill of rational doings: there is no nonsense about us, and our souls perish respectably. Liberate us, O Smirt, from the never-ending tyranny of our common-sense! Yet do you have a care that the door of our treadmill be left open, so that we may be returning at will to the gray round of its genteel reiterancies. For we do not desire to live always with irony; we do not want your wit and fancy along with our morning coffee, thank you very much; and it would be a most upsetting thing did the unveiled face of beauty come prying into our office hours. Only when we have nothing of real importance to attend to can the well-thought-of delight in art's foolishness."

Now when Smirt heard this appeal, he looked at his admirers with some natural pride, and he opened his mouth affably. But before he could speak he became aware of an incredibly beautiful blonde princess, dressed in white silk, and wearing upon her forehead a huge pearl hung from a silver circlet.

She had touched his arm, saying:

"So! And will you trifle with the public at large, Smirt, as lightly as you trifled with me?"

"I am sorry," Smirt answered, with frank regret, because he had not ever seen anywhere a creature more lovely; "I know there was once a princess. But I do not remember you."

*   *

ELEVEN

THE BLONDE PRINCESS

*

You must permit me then (the blonde princess replied) to recount the history of our acquaintance. It
dates back a great many years, to the time when I was
but a child, and indeed remained still a virgin. For
although profoundly corrupted in nature, and
though since infancy I had dreamed of the most subtle depravities, I had not lost that which the imaginative might call my innocence at the age of fourteen
years. I had been content until that time with de-
bauches of the fancy and with unshared pleasures
such as well-brought-up girl children induce only in
private.

You came now and then to visit our palace, but at
first you paid me no attention. Nevertheless I felt
drawn toward you, and I regarded you furtively at all
times. I thought continually about your manly beauties, and the thought led me into many solitary ex-
cesses of a nature I need not discuss.

A little later you permitted yourself to take minor liberties, such as tweaking my ear, or shaking playfully my immature breasts, or chucking me under the chin. When you met me in the Hallway of Lions or when I went with you to the palm garden, you would thus tease or caress me laughingly, even in the presence of the King my father, who saw no evil, peace be to his ashes!

I wished nothing better than to acquiesce in your impudence toward one in my exalted station. I shuddered with desire to know what thing in me and in my royal blood was in movement whenever you touched me. I observed you with never failing interest. . .Indeed, I can well recall that one day, in speaking to my sublime father about the wounds you had received in the war against Carthage, you offered to show him a scar which you had on your person, and for which you had avenged yourself by splitting the skull of the Nubian mercenary who inflicted it. I modestly withdrew from the apartment. But after passing through the doorway I paused, I looked back, and peeping between the curtains, I continued to observe you with interest. You unbuttoned your trousers and to my great joy displayed a magnificent thigh, bronzed and gleaming, overgrown with black wavy hairs, and traversed by a long rose-colored scar, which seemed to me very pretty in the dark flesh and the black hairs which surrounded it. I greatly wished to see what remained hidden under your shirt, but it was impossible to perceive anything definitely.

I had no affection for you, yet I desired to be crushed, to be conquered, to be defiled by you, Smirt, though it were but for a few moments. Girls have these passing fancies. So whenever you looked at me after the day I saw your naked hairy thigh, I was deeply stirred; I blushed; and when you touched me I shuddered with pleasure.

You invited me to visit your library. I came full of hunger for an adventure which would be tangible, and so might perhaps rid me of desires which, because they were not yet satisfied, had assumed unpleasant proportions and gave me no peace.

I was not destined to inspect your wealth of rare first editions and of the inscribed books presented to you by their admiring authors, nor was I to delight in your wittily derogatory comments upon such of these writers as were your personal friends. For before showing me these books, you exhibited to me your home at large, and so led me into your bedroom. Upon entering this intimate chamber, all closed and quiet, and smelling so delightfully of soap and cigarette smoke and leather, I was as if stupefied. My alarms, my curiosities, and my hopes, now aroused in all my body such violent palpitations that I was half suffocated, and I felt my hands and feet to be very cold.

You caused me to sit upon a red-covered sofa; you sat beside me; and in the while that with your customary ease and elegance you talked about stamp collecting and the fiscal policy of Napoleon, you laughed continually with an unnatural and constrained air. Your eyes had become so strange that I was both afraid and enchanted. I did not know what to say. I was ashamed, and I became red as a sunset.

By-and-by you squeezed each of my hands. With your fore-finger you tickled the palm of my hand, very gently; and drawing me into your lap, you commenced to kiss me upon the ear, murmuring and whispering so indistinctly that I understood nothing. The room was now silent. All seemed unbelievably silent. I could hear only my own heart beating frantically.

For a little while I remained motionless upon your knees, while your right arm embraced me, and you continued to kiss lightly my hair, my cheeks, my neck. I felt myself dying of pleasure, for never had I experienced such delight. But now your left hand had strayed indiscreetly, and it thus provoked new ardors. You questioned me in a voice so hoarse that I was frightened.

I could not answer at first, so much was I troubled.

I said by-and-by that you ought to be ashamed of yourself.

You arose then, you went to turn the key in the door, you drew down the shades of three windows nearly to the bottom, and you returned to me, who panted with shame, with terror, and with desire. You began to undress me in the twinkling of an eye, with hot hands that ran fondly over my bared flesh. You knelt to take off my shoes; upon arising you removed also my chemise and my drawers, which were of the quaint old full-bottomed pattern then worn by all women. Afterward, lifting your willing victim in both arms, you carried me like a sacrifice toward the altar of your bed. I regarded it as a sample of your forethought that the coverlets of this bed were already hospitably turned down.

Need I continue? To particularize the ensuing events would require a peculiarly Gallic touch: and the French themselves have the proverb, *La femme assez sait qui sait vivre et se taire.* Or, as the Scots phrase it, She kens muckle wha kens when to haud her tongue. All modern languages, in fine, preserve, in one or another variant, the sage Latin saying, *Mulier sapit qui pauca loquitur.* Since I believe this sentiment to be alike wise and applicable to this special stage of my narrative, I shall now honor this sentiment.

And in fact it appears sufficient to remark that the brief pain which you gave you repaid with a dozen delights. It seemed to me that I drowned in pleasure. Yet many of your doings astonished my inexperience, especially, I remember, when at the supreme moment of our first encounter you bellowed gently, like a refined bull. When you arose, at last, combing back your dishevelled dark curls with your fingers, and uttering deep sighs of satisfaction, I too was content.

After we had bathed and dressed carefully, so as to abstain from all appearance of evil, as the Apostle Paul has directed, then I regarded myself in your mirror. I was impressed with the strange and almost frightening beauty which I had at this moment. My face was flushed delicately, my lips were as red as though stained with wet blood, and my eyes glittered with an inhuman lustre. I was proud of myself. I exulted both in the pleasure which I had received and in that which I had given.

You made me promise not ever to return to your embraces, so that the memory of our debauch might endure in untarnished splendor; and this I did promise, with all my heart. I had never known a day more glorious or happy: it seemed to me I had begun to live only during the one hour and twenty-five minutes which I had passed in your convivial and educative bed; but I knew those eighty-five minutes could not ever be recaptured. Besides, at no instant did I feel for you any affection.

You came no more to the palace. I did not see you again. It occurred to me that my sublime father had perhaps caused you to be executed, after the usual tortures; but so taxing had become the ever widening range of my anatomical studies, under an efficient corps of varied instructors, that I lacked time to inquire into this matter.

Such, Smirt, was the history of our acquaintance.

When the blonde princess had finished her recital, Smirt frowned a little. He shook his head.

"I am sorry," he said, "but I do not remember you, at this present stage in my dream. The scar exists; but it was not given by a Nubian mercenary. There are yet other discrepancies in your story, alike of archæology and of local color, as well as, I modestly admit, of arithmetic. Still more perplexing, however, is the fact that you describe your release from technical virtue with an exactitude and a convincing truthfulness which prove you not to be female."

"Why, Smirt, but whatever nonsense are you talking? Is this the bosom of a man? Do you feel here the thighs of a man? Or for that matter—"

"Pardon me," Smirt said, withdrawing his hand,

"but I am to be convinced in this delicate affair neither by sight nor touch, nor by any other of my senses. I prefer to be guided by experience."

"And yet in a tête-à-tête, Smirt, no Southern gentleman ought to begrudge the evidence of his senses."

"Nevertheless," Smirt replied, "I can remember seducing no young woman who did not afterward contend—quite as though I had not been present during the whole transaction—that I had either persuaded her against her will or brutally overpowered her resistance. I can recall no gentlewoman into whose life I have brought romance who did not display afterward, more or less volubly, this quaint hallucination. You do not display it: and I deduce, as a sound logician, that you are not female."

The princess stared at him, smiling a little oddly. You saw that the large pearl she wore upon her forehead had altered in its coloring: for it glowed now like a ruby.

And Smirt continued to speak with extreme and careful politeness:

"No, I do not remember you. I can but suggest that during the prolonged career of a Peripatetic Episcopalian one necessarily forgets much. There need be no personal side to such forgetfulness. I do not remember you: that is all. Nor do I quite understand, my dear sir, why you should have enkindled in every part of your body to this fiery red color, and have sprouted two horns and a very long forked tail— Why, but what the devil!"

"Formerly," agreed the so remarkably transformed princess, "I was called that. But what with the progress of science and of scepticism, and the need to cut down our operating expenses, and the great popularity of mergers, affairs have been altered."

TWELVE

* *

—— & COMPANY

*

As the junior partner," the appalling fiend continued, "it is a part of my duties to relieve the old gentleman of all these routine affairs in the way of temptation and carnality and so on. Yes, Smirt, we have conducted business for a long while now as All-Highest & Company."

The speaker and Smirt were at this instant sitting astride upon a flash of lightning, confronting each other, so that Smirt journeyed face forward, and the scarlet devil courteously rode backwards, as these two travelled with a great and yet almost unremarkable rapidity through space. They encountered no wind, since between the stars there is no atmosphere. Smirt had thus no actual feeling of movement; and it seemed to him a rather odd thing, this sensation of sitting quite still on a flash of lightning.

Yet he saw that above and below, and on every side of Company and Smirt, glittered various constellations, and all these appeared constantly to shift in position and to pass away, so quickly travelled the flash of lightning through endless space. And Smirt noted yet another odd thing: the right foot of Company was human, but the left foot was shaped like the hoof of a goat.

"Let us distinguish," said Smirt, when he had wholly got his bearings: "for I was not tempted in the least."

Red Company shrugged. "And why should you be, Smirt, with so many plump and juicy young women about, as alike as peas in a pod to begin with, and to end with, as alike as wives in a bed? I blushed, I assure you, to be tempting anybody of your wide experience and savoir faire with such trumpery bait; but the old gentleman has in these matters His own notions. Unprogressive, I fear. And even these notions I bungled. So you saw through me, of course. You caught at once my slight slip in feminine psychology, because you understand women better than I do."

"Oh, that, Company, that is a mere matter of experience. You should see more of them, that only is needed. Indeed it occurs to me that, with a little more experience of women, you might find women of a decided usefulness in your own province, of stirring up disquiet and wickedness among men."

"I shall make a note of that, Smirt," said the fiend gratefully; and he produced a small red note-book with a red pencil. "Meanwhile I am flustered. Your acumen has quite dumbfounded me at the moment I was going on to offer you strange sins and infamous pleasures and all the subtler refinements of abominable love. Oh, just the usual routine! There is no need to go into it now. To the contrary, it is a relief to me to be spared such uncongenial nonsense. The old gentleman writes all those speeches, I must tell you. He reads Oscar Wilde a great deal."

"Why, then, since your evil devices have failed, to what cause, Company, should I attribute the pleasure of your company, or perhaps," Smirt continued, with his unfailing flair for that variousness which is the life of prose, "perhaps one had better say of your society, on this flash of lightning?"

"It is merely that, since our management of Earth does not please you," replied Company, as he indicated a planet now only some few million miles ahead of them, "you have here a specimen of our later style of work, which we would be delighted to present with the firm's compliments."

"And what would I do with that planet, Company?"

"Why, whatsoever you elected, Smirt, now that you have baffled my diabolical arts and retain the

old gentleman's pocket piece. For that, I must tell
you, confers omnipotence—within limits."

"Oh, I see. The coin is a talisman which confers
omnipotence—within limits. That is quite convenient."

Thereupon Smirt took out of his pocket the forty
reis piece, and he wished for a package of cigarettes.
How it happened there is no telling, but straightway
the coin lay in Smirt's hand on top of a package of
cigarettes which Smirt regarded with chill disapproval. Not even in the matter of smoking did these
divine beings appear intelligent.

"Plain Virginia tobacco—along with a box of
matches, please," said Smirt long-sufferingly; and at
once his will was accomplished.

Then Smirt resumed his conversation with the
Lord of Evil, saying: "Why good tobacco should ever
be degraded with a mixture of Turkish tobacco is
more than my limited imagination has yet been able
to conceive. No, Company: I appreciate your offer,
and I thank you most heartily for these cigarettes.
But for me to exercise my omnipotence—even within
limits—over any planet, would involve my becoming
the God of that planet. It would mean responsibility.
No; I very much prefer to criticize, and to disparage
urbanely, the conduct of a world for which someone
else is responsible."

"That is true, Smirt, as we have often learned to our cost. Ah, but what dashing epigrams you have made about both good and evil with that fine urbanity of yours!"

"Oh, but come now," Smirt comforted Company, "there was nothing personal intended. In all I have written as to your universe, I, as an Episcopalian, believed—in so far of course as any absolute conviction is permitted to an Episcopalian—that neither member of your firm existed. So none of my wit and fancy and erudition was consciously aimed at either of you. I simply did not know of your existence, far less of your consolidation; but we live and learn."

"In fact, as the hair dwindles, Smirt, the wits increase."

Smirt looked at his dreadful companion for a moment. Smirt lighted a cigarette, and Smirt said,—

"You remind me, Company, of a good story that is going the rounds."

"Then let us have it, Smirt, for my sense of humor is devilish keen."

"Stop me if you have heard this," Smirt urged; and he continued:

"A good story is going the rounds about a skittish banker, whose hair, in spite of all his precautions, is beginning to grow thin. His partner in business, it seems, was summoned to the telephone late one evening, and under the impression that this was a long-distance call, did not answer—"

"Ah, yes," said Company, "but all partners are like that. I know them. For I too have a partner; and between ourselves, Smirt, I sometimes think I might just as well have a palsy."

"You surprise me, Company—"

"Oh, He has many sterling qualities, Smirt. I would be the last person to criticize my collaborator. Some people are simply born scatter-brained and muddled, and there is no doing anything whatever about it."

Here again, Smirt reflected, was the auctorial temperament: but with his usual modesty, Smirt (in continuing his anecdote) refrained from all comment.

"He thought little of it at the time," Smirt went on, "not having noticed anyone in the hallway. Only two days later, however, after the police had been most reluctantly called in, a sedate and personable young manicurist, with an uncommonly fine head of naturally blonde hair—"

"Oho!" said Company, winking, "but now I see. And I know that sort of young woman from her boots up as far as one usually goes."

"—Was arrested in St. Louis," Smirt continued: "and after having been questioned rigorously, confessed she had nothing to do with the robbery, but had nevertheless attempted to score off her too amorous employer in this startling fashion."

Company laughed over this anecdote with such fervor as to incur grave danger of tumbling off the flash of lightning. He said, as he wiped away his tears with a red handkerchief:

"That is human nature, all over. I see a great deal of it in my own work. Yes, that is not only a very funny story. It is an instructive story. I must remember to tell the All-Highest that story,—though, between ourselves, Smirt, humor is not His strong point."

"You surprise me," Smirt stated, "upon at least two grounds."

"He has many sterling qualities, Smirt. But, no, humor is not one of them, just between ourselves. However, let us say no more about this little defect, Smirt, and—to go back in our conversation—we shall trust by-and-by to have the benefit of your yet further criticism and of your damned urbanity also."

"Of my what, Company?" Smirt asked, surprised.

"Ah, but in my mouth, Smirt, the adjective 'damned' is, as you will readily see, a great compliment, since it represents my *beau idéal* in all matters."

"Yes, that is true. I quite understand. And it will be a pleasure, Company, to help you out in any possible way with my experience, my savoir faire, and indeed, if I may so, with my reputation. If people knew that I was interested in your universe, and that I had consented in some sort to supervise it, why, that, you see, well, it would get you a certain following among the very cognoscenti who just now make fun of your universe. It would give you a *cachet*, a prestige, and in brief an æsthetic *je ne sais quoi*."

The fiend regarded Smirt reflectively, with a smile of frank pleasure. Company said,—

"You are kind, Smirt, with an unlooked-for condescension which I can but humbly describe as incredible."

"I am always incredible, Company, because I believe in myself. That is virtually a lost art in these days of democracy and of altruism and of other herd-making devices."

"In short—you are Smirt."

"That is my métier. But, to go back a little—in regard to the planet you offered just now—I must point out, for your own good, my dear fellow, that in the firm's place, I would have made the planet a perfect sphere. It is an ungrateful task to look a gift planet in the polar regions. Still, that flattening at each polar region, it really is an error in taste. It is not graceful. Form, my dear Company, form is

86

the first consideration in every branch of art. The thing lacks symmetry."

The red fiend fetched out his red note-book. He said:

"Now that you draw my attention, Smirt, I can see what you mean. I shall make a note of it. And I regret that we should have picked out for you a seemingly imperfect piece of workmanship—"

"Oh, not at all, my dear Company! I accept planets in the spirit in which they are offered. It is a rule with me."

"—And besides, the irregularity is very slight."

This touched upon heresy. Smirt at once became grave. He remarked gravely:

"In art there are no trifles. Through continued attention to trifles, in that way alone, may perfection be, not ever reached, to be sure, my dear sir, but adumbrated."

"I shall make a note of that also, Smirt—for our future guidance."

"And for another matter, Company, the planet lacks distinction. It is shaped, I mean, exactly like any other planet; it is ornamented with the usual continents and oceans; and the trite moon attends it. Your firm really does fall rather into a rut, sir, I am afraid, when I consider the thousands of quite similar planets which you have already produced."

The fiend wriggled under the continued candor of Smirt's criticism. And Company now said, to defend himself:

"But it is the All-Highest, Smirt, who attends to the designing and to cosmology in general. He has many sterling qualities, let us remember. I do not say that inventiveness is one of them. And at His age every artist has necessarily formed his style."

"That is true," said Smirt, "even when the style ambles in unabashed mediocrity; and I have no doubt that, after all, the firm has done its best. One should not, perhaps, in strict fairness, ask more. Nevertheless, for your own good, I must warn you that among the better class of critics mere repetition is not esteemed. It is not seemly that space should be thus cluttered up with planets as indistinguishable from one another as the books of an aging novelist."

At that, Company produced once more his small red book.

"I shall make yet another note, Smirt, of the fact that you wish the physical universe altered from beginning to end; and we will of course weigh the suggestion with due care."

"And for another matter, Company, now that we are upon the topic of evil, and since it has thus cropped up of itself, as it were, as naturally as original sin—"

"But were we indeed upon the topic of evil, Smirt?"

"Obviously, my dear sir, since both you and I are even now talking about it. Evil, as I was about to note with regret when you interrupted me—oh, but no apologies are necessary!—evil is not what it used to be; and all human wickedness tends to deteriorate in its quality. Now I hold no brief for evil: quite possibly, from an ethical point of view, it would be as well to abolish evil, howsoever unsettling might be the resultant disemployment of former members of the police force, of the bar, and of the judiciary. That, you understand, is a matter concerning which I reserve opinion. I note merely, sir, that evil is your province. My point is merely that so long as you, Company, continue to supply the world with evil, it should be your pride as an artist to furnish a somewhat superior grade to that now in use."

The fiend had opened his little red book yet again, asking,—

"And what do you suggest, Smirt—?"

"I suggest that the first step, the really decisive step, is to effect a complete change in our modern style of dress. It cannot possibly have escaped your notice that since men took to wearing dull colors their crimes have become equally dull."

"That is perhaps true. But even so—"

"In a sack suit, in a suit just such as he knows some hundreds of other men to be wearing," Smirt went on, "a criminal will instinctively hold up, and rob the cash register of, a shoe store or a filling station, he will forge a cheque, he will rape a trained nurse, or he will commit some other folly equally vulgar and un-exhilarating. Yet when suitably costumed, let us say, in a scarlet and gold doublet, or if given a neat crown and a robe of imperial purple—when made properly conspicuous, I repeat—that same misguided person might well become a Borgia or a Nero, and sin quite handsomely."

"I do not deny that, Smirt. It is only that this theory—"

"This established rule, my dear fellow. I recall an instructive instance, now that you continue to harp on this topic. An acquaintance of mine, a dentist, had lived sordidly for years upon the petty miseries of his clients, until one Christmas morning, when his wife gave him a handsome dressing gown very richly striped with blue and silver. She insisted that he wear it about the house during the holidays, and he humored her. He had been married for some time. But upon New Year's eve, my dear sir, he removed from the parlor mantel an onyx clock, and with this clock he battered out his wife's brains. That was not a great crime, I admit; there was about it nothing grandiose:

yet it did have a neat touch of originality and of grotesque poetry, as it were, which the man had never displayed in filling teeth or in any of his bridgework; and it must be imputed—as indeed the coroner's jury did impute it—to his unaccustomedly rich attire."

"No doubt, Smirt, you are right. Yet I would submit—"

"Ah, but to what end, my dear fellow, when I am supported everywhere by zoölogy? For do you but observe the animal kingdom! It is the sheep, the rabbit, and the ignoble hyena who wear dull colors, where the tiger, the leopard, and the serpent go splendidly attired. These last-named feel themselves to be properly conspicuous; they ravage therefore with élan. They sin handsomely."

"Still, Smirt—"

"I perceive your argument, Company. I follow you. It is wholly true that the larger birds of prey do not ever wear bright colors, and that the shark also might seem, to the superficial, to affect unostentation. But that, my dear fellow, that is because the one of these great criminals practises his profession in the bedazzling gold and blue of high heaven, and the other among the crimson coral reefs and the million-hued resplendent tropic seaweeds. Their sombreness among all this splendor thus lends to them just that sense of being conspicuous which, rather than mere brightness, the criminal needs to inspire him. Their sombreness, I would put it, compels the eye quite as inevitably as does the mourning garb of Hamlet at the gay court of Denmark."

"*Hamlet!* yes, I remember *Hamlet*," replied Company. "*Hamlet* is by Shakespeare. Shakespeare is the greatest of all writers of English."

"In his time, my dear sir," Smirt answered; and he so fell into a sudden silence.

"But, Smirt, that is what everyone tells me—that Shakespeare is still the greatest of all writers of English. I am not like the old gentleman: I have written no book, and I do not pretend to be literary, you understand."

"And I do not argue the matter, Company. I know that many persons affect to admire the writings of that—of that person. Tastes differ: some few of us have learned to appreciate the delicacies and the splendors of prose writing as an actual art: and that is all."

Now the fiend looked at Smirt, for an instant, with a grin which Smirt did not like especially. But Smirt did not say anything further to this scarlet ignoramus; and if Smirt seemed a trifle stately and reserved, it was for a sufficient reason.

"Your suggestions as to iniquity also shall be duly considered," said Company, after making an entry in his little red book, "and in my modest way, I shall trust to profit by them. In the mean time," he continued, just as the flash of lightning struck the ground noiselessly, and so vanished with every bit of Company except his voice, "in the mean time, this, I believe, is your grave, where I was instructed to leave you."

PART THREE

BEYOND TWO TOMBS

＊　　＊

＊

"*Even during the Han Period learned Confucian writers believed that prosperity, erudition and high official rank were secured by giving to one's ancestors grave-sites on which they could look with satisfaction and gratitude. The* lin, *or unicorn, is related to have appeared in China from time as a harbinger of good government, or at the birth of a virtuous ruler.*"

* *

THIRTEEN

AT SMIRT'S GRAVE

*

It surprised Smirt, thus to be standing at his own grave. Yet the range of his first disquiet was soon checked by the discovery that he and his wife had self-evidently been buried in this place a great while ago. It followed that for him to be upset, at this late date, by the deaths of these people would be out of all reason. Why, but he and Jane, to judge by these very old-looking tombstones, and by the gray spider webs which were about each grave, must have lain here undisturbed for several hundred years. As a close student of human nature, Smirt knew that no human grief can outwear a century. He inferred, as a sound logician, that the emotion of which he was now conscious could not be grief.

"And besides," he reflected, "it is likely that Smirt has a great many graves. The blonde princess knew me in what I can but assume to be an earlier incarnation. I have no doubt lived in many such incarna-

97

tions. In fact, I can now perceive, dimly, that ever since time began—or at all events, ever since urbanity first came into being—the Peripatetic Episcopalian has followed, upon his discreet path midway between piety and atheism, after that beauty which does not exist; he has hungered in all eras for the impossible, irrespective of any moral ambition; and continually his own self-sufficiency has slain him. In every land lies the grave of Smirt, who could not ever be content with the half-handed and humorless doings of All-Highest & Company, Ergo, I cannot display any special emotion over any special one of my multitudinous graves without exhibiting undue favoritism."

Smirt looked up toward heaven, pensively. He directed thither an urbane smile; and Smirt said:

"The dull-mindedness of Your futile and charming world, All-Highest, has yet again disposed of me, unavailingly. For I still survive, You may note. And from my most recent graveside I remark that when You gave man reason, he did but cease to believe in You: there was no great hurt done, either way. But You granted him imagination also. You permitted him to create in his dreams another world than Your world. He became then Your critic, for it was apparent to him that his inventions went beyond Your inventions."

98

Smirt waved a protesting hand to forestall any divine reply. "In all humbleness, sir, I admit that my notions may be wrong: but I cannot believe they are wrong. A thunderbolt would not, I can assure You, convince me, and any such display of brute force would but lay You open to the charge of peevishness. Besides that, I really do think quite favorably of Your inventions, so far as they go. I have delighted in Your world: for its beauty, its curiousness, and its unintentional humor, I give all thanks. But my heart I have given to the world which I create in my dreams."

He looked down, toward the grave of his wife. "And to you also, my dearest, my heart was given."

After that, Smirt said: "You should be a proud woman, Jane, that after I do not know how many years your husband is lamenting you. You have been dead now for a great while. It was not this afternoon that you went out to play contract bridge with the Ralston girls. It was in a faraway time you left me, for your tombstone is very old. I regret that faraway time."

Smirt said: "And I have but one complainment to make against you, or it may be four complainments. You could not let a fire alone: you must forever be poking at it, and you needed to be pulling it about, until there was no fire, but only the remnants of a

99

fire. And when my shirts and my underclothes came back from the laundry you would not put them at the bottom of the pile, so that I could wear my shirts and my underclothes in a regular rotation. And besides that, you would not put your own shoes down in a sensible way, either, after you took them off: you put always the left shoe on the right side, and the right shoe on the left, so that I was continually straightening after you."

He blinked a little, wondering at this unaccountable moistness of his eyes.

And Smirt said then: "But my fourth complainment is that you never permitted me to wish I was married to somebody else. You made of me a man who did not have but one wife, and at times that made me wonder if I could be a real genius? There was no other distinguished writer, and there was no famous artist of any kind, but had his third wife, or perhaps his fifth wife, and was getting on with her so very badly that he would soon have another wife. But I had only you, my dearest, and I desired only you; and your common-sense made me over into as good a husband as could be expected."

He considered that fact with frank wonder. Yes, he had been an excellent husband.

And Smirt said also: "You were a wise woman, Jane. It did not matter to you that in my mind I was unfaithful and followed after a beauty which does not exist. You knew that mere human thinking does not amount to much, after all. You knew that men were very often up to such nonsense. It was a thing which you had to put up with, like dentists, and like rainy weather, and like traffic policemen. You did not bother about such male talk and male foolishness. You did not care at all that I made mirth and beauty; you would have liked it better if I had made shoes or sermons or prescriptions; but, as matters fell about in this imperfect world, the genius of your husband was a matter which you had to put up with; so you condoned it loyally. You made me as good a wife as could be expected."

And finally Smirt said: "It is very right that when the tourists and the lovers of fine literature come here to weep over the grave of Smirt they must weep over your grave also. It is proper that every biographer should put a picture of you in all my biographies, and that the orators should speak nicely about you at my centenaries until time ends. So do I cry out to you, my dearest, who have been dead now for a great long while, Hail and farewell!"

Then only did Smirt perceive those persons who had surrounded him.

*   *

FOURTEEN

THE PUBLIC STILL AT LARGE

*

It was on the top of a bleak mountain, seemingly, that Smirt, pausing in soliloquy, looked up from the two graves. He saw that some fourteen persons had gathered about him, in a gray twilight; and the butcher said:

"The more the merrier. Smirt is in our midst. Polly put the kettle on! Never had I hoped to find among us that genius who depicts with such utter loveliness, such impish wit, and such tender humanity, man's endless searching after the golden dream which he creates for himself."

"Pleased to meet you, Smirt," said the baker. "You must promise to pay us a nice long visit. I never saw you looking better. Anyone with a soul to appreciate beauty will find in countless pages of your books that which no other living writer can offer."

And the candlestick maker remarked: "Now, but this is a pleasure! I admire your style as much as I deplore your morals. Yet both of us bring light into dark places; and all men of ability should know one another."

"But this is affecting," Smirt exclaimed; "for it is you, my admirers, who have gathered at this graveside!"

Tom answered him: "You bet your bottom dollar. Have a look at the real Simon Pure."

"None others need apply," said Dick. "We are the public at large. We only are the lords of distinguished persons; and we agree, just now, that your books are whimsical, elfin, and even romantic, without being banal."

And Harry said confidentially: "Trademark blown on each bottom. Your writings are pure and beneficent. A Boston policeman can read your collected works without a blush. The most innocent maiden of fifteen can read any book of yours from cover to cover and then lay it down completely disappointed."

"And how, my admirers, are you called in this planet?"

"We are roses by any other name," replied Madame Quelquechose. "But a few great persons know that we rule over them, the poor fish. Each of these fish, when he had perceived our omnipotence, became insane."

"The fish went cuckoo," Señora Etcetera explained.

103

"Cuckoo, jug-jug-jug, tirili-lio, caw-caw, tweet-tweet-tweet, cluck, quack-quack! No sane fish has ever dared to think about our idiocy."

"And do we worry?" asked Lady Ampersand, contemptuously. "We who alone are eternal and almighty are not honored in public by the well-thought-of. Which shows that twice two makes hay while the sun shines. Polly put the kettle on! But for my part, I find in the sex experience greater possibilities for acquiring insight than in any other experience. Why should not you and I, Smirt, now step into those bushes for the purpose of discovering reason, destiny, or what you will, and thus solve the riddle of the universe?"

"Am I to understand, then," said Smirt, a little perturbed, "that you who admire me are not wholly right in the head?"

Anon answered him, leering and mowing: "We see all, hear all, know all, invent all, and exalt all. We dethrone also. Our sanity beggars description. We think, just now, that your books are very deep. One needs quite a knowledge of world literature and mythology to understand them."

"Our sanity must be seen to be appreciated," Ibid cried out. "Make an appointment. Line forms to the right. We have neuroses and radios, but what has become of those old-fashioned winters? I would rank your books among the better-class fantasies in all modern literature."

"I really cannot report," said Smirt, "that the management of this planet is completely satisfactory if you ladies and gentlemen be my only admirers hereabouts."

"I think your books are perfectly wonderful," said Mrs. Murgatroyd.

"We regard you as one of our leading writers," declared the world. "You strike a responsive chord in the hearts of every type of reader."

"Oh, but you do put such cute things in your books!" said the world's wife. "How can any one person even write so many pretty books as you have written? I too once knew a poet. Oh, a beautiful poet! But he is dead now. Yes, quite dead! Yet I shall always treasure the poems he made up about me. Mr. World is not at all literary. Mr. World is a Puritan, without any *joie de vivre*. Do you compose on the typewriter?"

"It all depends," said Smirt,—"and, well, good-evening, everybody!"

They replied confusedly: "Do not leave us, Smirt! We are the true gods, but men dare not worship us openly, because of our feeble-mindedness. Great wits to madness are so near allied. Those false gods whom men pretend to hold in honor dwell very far beneath us. They are quite impossible persons. No gods are dependable except the public at large. What author, do you think, has most influenced you? You must pay us all a nice long visit, because rolling stones collect no moss. So you must teach us to regard man as a proletarian collectivist."

"But no, upon the whole, ladies and gentlemen, I think that I must be leaving you."

They became angry then, and joining hands, they all danced about Smirt in a circle, crying out in the gray twilight:

"What is that to us? Absence makes the heart grow fonder. You display a superlative egotism gone rank and stale, a pathetic vanity, and a smug self-satisfaction raised to a point beyond calculation. Polly put the kettle on! Smirt, Smirt, he deals in dirt! We think, just now, that you are, finally, unimportant. You buzz about in your season of sunshine, over your filthy little fantasies, like a blue-bottle fly over cow-dung."

"What is that?" Smirt exclaimed. "I do not follow your similes."

They replied: "But we, the public at large, we abide here, ruling over all that lives. Do have another cup of tea! Your prose is hopelessly artificial and over ornamented and self-conscious. We saw you in the old doctor's barnloft. But that was under another planet, and zero weather has crept south. So do you now tell us, without any more shilly-shally, what will be the future trend of literature in the South?"

Smirt did not answer them. Instead, Smirt had passed onward, unhurriedly, with complete dignity, to regard a young woman whose employment appeared unusual.

FIFTEEN

*   *

IS ABOUT TANA

*

It was a relief to have escaped from the public at large, into this pleasant upland. The pathway led by a cave; and at the cave's mouth, which was overgrown everywhere with the intermingled dark green and the light green of ivy, sat this woman, beside a fire of juniper wood. In her hand was a large fork, like a trident, with which she was toasting crescent-shaped cakes over this fire.

She looked up at Smirt. She smiled upon Smirt in the while that she asked his business in these parts.

"In all parts and at all times," he replied, "my business is of an odd nature. It is my business to crimp and to pressgang and to kidnap words. I marshal them upon paper. I then drill these words in a not ever ending full-dress parade."

"The fine books of Smirt," the young woman responded, still smilingly, "are noted in rumor, and they keep everywhere a famousness."

"So, you know me, Tana! or at least you know me by reputation. Come now, but that is gratifying; it is peculiarly gratifying, now that my grave is well covered over with spider webs, to find that Smirt is still known."

"I know you, Smirt, because I am served by the powers of the moon and by all else which is unstable and false and feeble. Since time began I have known you and your like, Smirt, and until time ends for you, frail Smirt, your thinking will not ever be unswayed by me."

"That is as it should be, Tana. You remain always in my thoughts because it is the business of every artist to contemplate the beautiful. That fact has already arrested my steps in this place. That fact has caused me steadfastly to remember that there was once a princess—a princess who, I now perceive, is also a good cook, for those cakes have a delicious appearance."

"These cakes," she told him, "are made of meal, of red wine, of salt, and of honey. Yet it is not truly these four things which I bake, and then toast, over this fire. I toast the blood and the body and the soul of the moon, so that the moon may have neither rest nor peace, and must suffer unendingly, until the moon grants me what I desire."

"In fact, Tana, when one deals with any of these

109

heavenly bodies, and especially with the moon, it is necessary to take a high hand and to stand up for one's rights jealously. Otherwise, there is no telling."

"That is true, Smirt—"

"—For one must bear in mind, my dear Tana, that the moon has an apogee."

"You astound me, Smirt—"

"The moon has also a perigee, a synodical period, and a mean daily motion. These are not matters to be trifled with, I submit. A prudent person will be circumspect in dealing with such endowments."

"That which you say seems wholly plausible, Smirt: and yet," the girl added, a little bewildered, "yet when I think about it, somehow, I do not believe it means anything."

"Why should it?" Smirt asked, reasonably.

"Because—why, because most persons do mean something when they talk."

"I cannot fully grant that statement—no, not as an axiom, Tana. And in any case, I am Smirt. I do not have anything to do with most persons. To the contrary, I am exclusive. I pick and choose my associates. For that reason, if for no other reason, you should regard it as a great compliment that Smirt has stopped here to chat with you."

Tana looked at him as if thoughtfully, for the space of two heartbeats; and then said,—

"Yet it might be better for you, Smirt, to go forward yonder, where the path forks to the right hand."

"And to what, pray, can that path conduct me, that I should be leaving Tana for the sake of it?"

"It will lead you, Smirt, to a small snug home, and to a tidy shop with a fair line of business, and to a woman; and all three of these will be yours for the asking."

But Smirt laughed aloud at these inducements. And Smirt said:

"What are such matters, Tana, to an artist who is reasonably sophisticated? Should I be leaving incarnate beauty for sordidly bourgeois delights? And whither, sweetheart, does that other path conduct one, where the path forks to the left hand?"

"That of course is a sinister path. And so, Smirt, that is a very little travelled path. For it turns away from use and wont and from human contentment, and from all other traps of the Spider Woman, entering into the fabulous city of Amit."

"Ah, ah! But it is in that place," said Smirt, drawing, with his habitual readiness, upon the vast stores of Smirt's erudition, "that the Stewards of Heaven reside."

"Yes, Smirt,—yet only for their allotted season."

"Well, but, Tana, it is needful there should be gods and gods, and then still other gods. It is good for

mythology. And yet none of them—do you know?—
none seems to be very intelligent. For I have weighed
the cosmic methods of All-Highest & Company, I
must tell you; and while I still hope to correct these
methods, I am not optimistic. Moreover, I have seen
the public at large, who mutter and bluster upon this
mountain top; and on the whole, Tana, I have seen
enough of the public at large."

Now the girl raised her hand in protest. Smirt saw
that the little finger was missing, or, rather, that upon
neither of Tana's hands had there ever been any little
finger.

"Let us not speak of the public at large," said Tana,
hastily. "Let us leave them in their high station un-
molested even by our thinking, since none may dethrone them. Let us honor, instead, the moon and
get our profit of moonshine."

"But," Smirt replied, doubtfully, "I was not looking for profit. I was looking for a legend."

"I have many legends, Smirt."

"Then let us have three of them."

The beautiful girl arose, putting aside her trident.
She entered the cave, crying out—

"Dr. Chronos, here is a patient for you!"

* *

SIXTEEN

CAVES MAKE THE CAVE-MAN

*

Now when Tana had entered her cave, she went to the black mantelpiece, and she tilted sidewise the black onyx clock (which must have been left over from the second anecdote that I related to Company, Smirt reflected), and in this way she stopped its ticking.

Smirt, following her with a quickness which appeared permissible in a widower of so many centuries' standing, saw before him a couch covered with robes of sable and ermine. The walls of the cave were hidden by silvery-colored hangings embroidered with black stars and black suns and black comets. Upon a seven-cornered table were set forth five kinds of fruit and black wine in three silver flagons. In this cave was a great quietness.

Then Tana said no. And there was not any moving her, Smirt found. She very resolutely continued to say no.

"No, for it is incredible!" said Tana. "It frightens me, you impudent huge monster!"

Afterward Tana said: "No, Smirt, but I could not possibly endure it! So do be still!"

Tana likewise said, in half stifled distress: "No, my friend, I repeat, no! No!..Ah!..Ouh!..Whew!.. Aïe!"

And besides that, Tana said, almost inaudibly: "No, sweetheart, but you go too far! Fie, sweetheart, stop, stop! ah, but do not stop! Oho, sweetheart, but you will be the death of me, sweetheart!"

You heard also, in this quiet cave, a gentle bellowing noise, such as might have been uttered by an unusually refined bull.

* *

SEVENTEEN

PATCHES OF MOONSHINE

*

So now, you obstreperous and shameless Smirt, do you sit down beside me, at my feet, like a pacified good child," said Tana, after she had thus denied Smirt, for the third time, copiously. "And let us both rest a little in the while that I speak of my legends."

She spoke then, without any haste, stroking the dark curls of his hair with formal gestures. Now the words of Tana resembled the humming of bees, they were like the sedate noise of a top turning round and round and round, ceaselessly. And they may well have been magic words, for it seemed to Smirt that this sound was the sound of a spinning-wheel upon which all the thread of his life was spun. It seemed to him that long years passed by, and went away from him forever, in the drone of this peace-giving noise and under the fond touch of those peace-giving deformed hands. Yet all the while the clock told him that the time did not change.

So was it that for one bewildering instant Smirt
got his profit of moonshine. For it seemed to him
during this instant that the magic of Tana conferred
on him four powers. It seemed to him that he at last
understood the voice of the wind, and knew how to
change water into wine, how to tame wild beasts, and
how to cure all diseases except curiosity. And it
seemed to him also that he went into dark places
where the Old Believers, men and women and small
children alike, supped together naked, eating peculiar foods which Smirt did not touch, and afterward
they danced their peculiar dances, and sang and made
music, and then made love, all in complete darkness,
so that no one of them knew the other. Yet the black
onyx clock upon Tana's black mantelpiece told Smirt
that the time remained twelve minutes after six, just
as though it were all happening upon the front page
of the *Herald Tribune*.

Smirt was well content with this manner of magic.
He knew, nevertheless, that he still sat at the feet of
Tana. He knew that all these matters were but a mo-
mentary illusion put upon him by the moon's power;
and he wondered whether it was done with the perigee or the apogee, now that the moon's ancient magic
had shown Smirt how to cure all diseases except
curiosity.

So he shrugged. He arose from the floor of the cave

gracefully; and, as became a sound logician, he started the black clock again.

Then Tana cried out, clasping together her three-fingered hands,—

"The wrong doctor has come for me!"

"My dear," said Smirt, "this is no medical man, but only a white rabbit, who, for all I know, has popped out of the pages of Lewis Carroll."

"No, Smirt, for it is the rabbit which lives at the foot of the cassia-tree, of the moon's own tree, forever pounding together those drugs which make the elixir of eternal life," replied the voice of Tana.

But Tana herself was no longer there. Instead, at the side of the white rabbit, a gray cat was scampering across the fields of this pleasant upland.

The black dog pursued neither of them. This black dog had a white muzzle and four white feet. He sat in Tana's deserted cave, looking up, with a complacence vaguely sinister, at the black mantelpiece, where a black onyx clock ticked relentlessly.

He looked then at Smirt. "We are now entering," said the black dog, "the city of Âmit, the home of the Stewards of Heaven. And much good may it do you!"

*   *

EIGHTEEN

FROM THE RADIATOR

*

For it may be," the black dog continued, "that in Amit Smirt will at last find his suitable audience to be composed of these divine beings who control an entire planet. It may be that this supernal audience will content Smirt."

"Black dog," said Smirt, "I was well enough content until you began to talk to me from the radiator in my writing room. For it was your talking, black dog, which first involved me in this nomadic sort of dreaming. It was your talking which has evicted me from the snug home wherein, I do not know how many centuries ago, I was comfortable enough with my wife and children and a steady income, and which has led me to wander about in unfamiliar places beyond my grave."

"Self preservation, Smirt," replied the black dog, "is the first law of nature."

"You put it trenchantly, black dog. You have a gift

118

for the striking, the novel phrase; and that is a fine gift."

"Bah!" said the black dog. "To begin with, I had to stand always on your radiator."

"In fact, I can imagine that to stand on a radiator, day in and day out, as your life's work, might pall after a while, even though I have never tried it myself."

"In the second place, Smirt, you continually filled me with bits of string."

"That does sound indigestible, I admit. And yet, even so, black dog—"

"But what is far worse, Smirt, I had to look at you all the time."

"Oh, come, but really now, black dog, I look at myself every day when I am shaving, and I cannot say I feel much the worse for it."

"The lather hides a great deal, Smirt. But nothing, nothing," said the black dog, with somewhat shaken composure, "can ever hide that smug self-conceit which you call your urbanity. And I had to watch that urbanity in action, every day, and all day. It was too much for any small wooden dog to endure; I began to feel that at any instant I might go mad and fly into splinters."

Smirt nodded, in sympathetic and complete understanding.

"Yes, yes," said Smirt, "it is true that urbanity does affect some people in that way. I have noticed it."

"So I did, Smirt, I did, in sheer desperation, point out that you lacked a suitable audience. Just as you put bits of string in me, Smirt, so did I put in you dissatisfaction; and exactly as you toasted me with your radiator, so did I grill you with the thought that two or three living persons were not talking about Smirt at that very moment."

"I see," said Smirt amiably; "you wanted to get rid of me."

"Your perceptiveness, Smirt, is astounding."

But Smirt waved aside this compliment, with his usual modesty. Smirt said:

"Oh, no, it is a mere matter of experience. I have noted that desire in yet other quarters. And I have encountered it not only in book reviews written by enviably young persons, black dog, but in grave magazine articles, and in books too, by people well advanced in senility. This getting rid of me is quite a national movement, which has at many times assumed the fervor of a crusade. Some day I must show you my press clippings. They will interest you. They will, as it were, buck you up. Oh, yes, beyond doubt they will, for a great number of these press clippings bear directly upon that same smug self-conceit about which you were just talking."

"This," said the black dog, "is beyond endurance!"

"To the contrary, black dog," Smirt consoled him, "my self-conceit is a popular superstition which any thoughtful person can well understand. It is a plain sample of *pseudodoxia epidemica*: and in its inevitability it outrivals by a great deal the question of the hare's sex, or the enigma of the lion's backward conduct in his amours, or even the vexed problem of Adam's navel—"

"Bah!" said the black dog.

"—For by the dull-minded," Smirt went on to explain courteously, "a person of any special talent is expected not to notice that he possesses this talent; by the dull-minded an artist is permitted to give over his life to his art, if he so elects, but he is not permitted to attach any ·audible importance to his art. Should he assume, in brief, in so many words, that his work is worth doing for its own worth, and is not merely a legalized form of prostitution, then that artist becomes a figure of fun. Oh, yes, one can quite understand that: and as a creative artist myself, in my own romanticizing way, I have often envied these imaginative flights of the dull-minded, which, in a democracy at least, are not ever hampered by rationality."

"Bah!" said the black dog.

"But you keep saying that, when Bow-wow would

be a welcome change, and upon the whole far more appropriate—"

"Bah!" said the black dog, "bah, bah! You talk and you talk. Bah! None the less you are still in search for that suitable audience of yours; and I have your writing room all to myself."

"In fact, black dog," said Smirt equably, "it is permitted you to remain standing on a radiator undisturbed; and it is permitted me to enter into the august presence of the Stewards of Heaven. I do not know as yet which one of us makes the nobler bargain, no, I do not know that absolutely; but I do know I have not any least desire to stand on a radiator."

"It is a pity," said the black dog, in a contained frenzy, "that I was made without teeth! There are times when I feel the need of them. However, I am in lively hopes the Spider Woman may finish the work I began."

Thus growling, he went back sulkily to his radiator; and Smirt entered the city of Amit with entire urbanity.

PART FOUR

TEACHES BY EXAMPLE

*   *

*

"According to Plutarch and Herodotus, the Mnevis of the Egyptians was held by some to be the mystic father of Apis. Again, in Deuteronomy XXVIII, we find 'the first fruits of the body' promised as one of the special blessings for obedience to the law. It will be remembered also that the oldest Spanish university, at Salamanca, was founded in 1240."

* *

NINETEEN

THE STEWARDS OF HEAVEN

*

The home of the Shining Ones was beautiful beyond imagining. It seemed not certain that even the refined and sinewy and multi-colored prose of Smirt could do full justice to Amit, now that in order to welcome Smirt, came from each of the seven palaces of Amit the tall master of that palace attended by his symbolic animal—excepting Phaleg, who came in red robes, like a much magnified cardinal, followed by a peacock.

Six of the Shining Ones wore eternal youth. Arathron, the Divine Father, alone kept the appearance, becoming to his estate, of a bearded man in early middle life whom a sedate mouse-colored goat accompanied everywhither. All were serene and handsome huge persons, and yet, as Smirt saw, they were impervious to humor. It was not possible to conceive that any one of them had ever laughed over anything which was not wholly stupid. The nobility of their faces and of their heroic forms and of their sublime dullness was a vague trouble to Smirt. These gods reminded him of a drove of superb cattle.

Such were the seven Stewards of Heaven, who said: "Homage to Smirt! Be very welcome to this place, to the eternal city of Amit. We have all heard of Smirt. Until to-day no fortunate one of us has beheld the face which is more admirable than the face of any god. To-day the bliss of the Shining Ones is made complete."

"Upon my word," Smirt reflected, "but these divine beings, if a little dull-minded, yet have big hearts, as well as a mighty civil way of putting matters."

"Now do you tell us," said Bethor, "what will be the future trend of Southern literature, what is your philosophy of life, and which one of your books do you like best."

"Well," Smirt replied, "I would say that all depends."

"Do you write in the morning or the evening?" asked Phaleg, "and does your secretary open all your letters? It must be simply wonderful to be a writer. Do you think that capitalism is doomed? What critic has best understood your work as a whole?"

"That, too, that all depends, my dear sir," Smirt assured Phaleg, "although I grant, of course, there is something to be said on the other side."

Then Och asked: "What author has most influenced you? Do you compose on a typewriter? If I were to tell you a perfectly true story about what happened to an aunt of mine would you like to make a book out of it? Why do you not write for the moving pictures?"

And thereafter, of course, the Shining Ones began to inquire about the younger Southern writers.

"Tell us frankly," said Phul (who was an hermaphrodite, clothed in pale green and pale yellow) "just what you think about DuBose Heyward, Roark Bradford, T. S. Stribling, Julia Peterkin, Hervey Allen, Thomas Wolfe, William Faulkner, and Paul Green. It must be simply wonderful to be a writer. What effect will the radio have upon literature?"

"Do you write every day," inquired Ophiel, "or do you wait for inspiration to move you? If I send you a book will you autograph it for a young man who is a close friend of my wife's third cousin, and who has already read one of your books? What do you usually have for breakfast when you are writing? How did you happen to take up writing as a profession? Do you really understand James Joyce?"

Hagith said: "When is your next book to appear? Are you working on anything just now? Have you devoted much study to Karl Marx? Who is Karl Marx? What are you going to call your next book?"

All the other usual questions did the huge Shining Ones ask with that benevolent inattention which befits the asking of these questions. Smirt began to feel quite at ease in the home of the Shining Ones, wherein every customary tribute was paid to the genius of a visiting writer. Everyone was abeam with delight, for all these divine beings had heard about Smirt's wonderful books from absolutely everybody, they told him, and they were all planning to read these books on the very first opportunity. Meanwhile, they had arranged in his honor a banquet; and Arathron, Smirt saw, had already risen to address the gods, as their toast-master.

* *

TWENTY

CONCERNS ROUTINE MATTERS

*

Continuing, Arathron remarked that he need say no more. He would add only that his endeavors to say anything whatever this evening had reminded the speaker of a story; which Arathron narrated. Like that Scotchman, gentlemen, your toast-master was unaccustomed to public speaking, though for a different reason. (*Laughter.*) He had been caught this evening quite unprepared by the arrival of Heaven's distinguished guest. (*Applause.*) This pleasant surprise, this highly pleasant surprise, had permitted the speaker no time for the preparation of any formal address, as in fact must be only too evident to his hearers. (*Cries of No, no!*) Arathron could but speak as the heart prompted: indeed, his present predicament reminded the speaker of a story; which Arathron narrated.

Well, and like that Irishman, gentlemen, the Stewards of Heaven had been afforded an unlooked-for pleasure. (*Prolonged applause.*) The speaker might make bold to say it was an exceedingly great pleasure. He would not, however, pursue his remarks along that line. It was sufficient to say they had among them one than whom no living writer, one in fact whose name was a household word among all lovers of a great and ancient art, for the speaker alluded to literature. (*Cheers.*) Literature, gentlemen, had its place, its esteemed place, in the life of every cultured person, and a special function that—inasmuch as no ladies were present—reminded the speaker of a story; which Arathron narrated.

It might be, the conclusion reached by the traveling man was not wholly logical. (*Loud laughter.*) It was not for the speaker to say. He could say boldly, however, without any fear of successful contradiction—

And Arathron did say it, at some length.

Smirt felt more and more at ease in the home of the Shining Ones, where every customary tribute was being paid to the genius of a visiting writer; so that, at the conclusion of Arathron's customary address, Smirt delivered, with his habitual ease and elegance, his customary impromptu acknowledgment. The brilliant, cordial, and engagingly modest observations of the guest of honor were greeted with all the customary applause.

Thereafter the Stewards of Heaven spoke of their own labors, in the while that the Shining Ones continued to partake of the banquet; for now Arathron was questioning his children as to how they had spent the day at their offices as the Stewards of Heaven. And they answered him, belching reverently.

Bethor replied first. He was by much the largest of the seven Stewards; he was of a golden color; he was clothed in sea-green and purple; and at his gold-shod feet crouched a lion. Two thousand and nine hundred legions of salamanders served under Bethor in the daily labors of his office. Now Bethor told about how he had caused zero weather to creep south, and had caused four lives to be claimed in feud war, with five wounded, and had caused Congress to meet in heated session.

Hagith talked next. Hagith was pink and plump and golden-haired: he was the most friendly looking of all the Stewards. He dressed in white and very light blue; he wore upon his breast an engraved tablet of burnished copper; a white bull lay beside him. Four thousand legions of undines were at Hagith's command. Hagith and his undines had during the term of that day split a French cabinet, and they had displayed storm warnings along the coast, as far as Cape Hatteras, and they had led a worried mother to slay son and self. All in all, it had been somewhat an off-day, devoted entirely to routine work, Hagith reported modestly.

Then Phaleg spoke. He was of a ruddy color, wearing scarlet; and a peacock attended him. Phaleg ruled over those thirty-five principalities which the gnomes inhabit. That day the red troops of Phaleg had compelled a banker to be flayed in quiz, and a gangster to go jestingly to death chair, and an irate husband to surprise couple in love nest.

Each one of the huge children of Arathron spoke with just that quiet air of self-reliance which befitted a hardworking and somewhat humorless Steward of Heaven, by whom even the most trivial and most tedious duties of his station were discharged conscientiously. But this was their hour of relaxation. So they jested heavily over their celestial banquet, becoming more and yet more befuddled as the Stewards swilled down the dark beer of Sekmet, until they had all reached a state of dignified and complete incoherence. This beer, to Smirt's personal taste, was unattractively seasoned, with mandrakes and with human blood, so that Smirt did not partake of it, nor did he eat any of the banquet.

In brief, the Stewards of Heaven drank out the evening as conscientiously as throughout the day they had worked, giving to the pleasures of the table their proper therapeutic place in the economy of divine living. They thus drugged themselves into a restful stupor with the dark beer of Sekmet. They now sprawled in their great gold and ivory chairs, snoring. But pallid Ophiel, who was dressed in black and azure, had fallen out of his chair, and lay flat on the floor, where his attendant buffalo served as a pillow.

Smirt only remained awake and alert in the eternal city of Amit.

*　　*

TWENTY-ONE

EPILOGUE OF SOBRIETY

*

Smirt alone remained awake and alert, and wholly
sober, in the eternal city of Amit; and he regarded the
insensible large overlords of this place a bit ruefully.
Drunkenness Smirt did not mind in particular, since
his long residence in a land given over to the barbari-
ties of Prohibition had made Smirt familiar with
drunkenness: but he did think it sad that to-morrow
every one of these immortal beings would be at his
office, seeing to it that a biplane plunged near Golden
Gate, or that a bishop rapped modern tendencies, or
that forty-three women's dresses, formerly to $16.50,
should be $5.00.

Yes; Smirt found it all a little sad, and a trifle perplexing: yet, since the Stewards of Heaven were only
realists, their doings, he decided, as he sat in urbane
sobriety among these divine drunkards, did not really
matter. Such doings did not enter into the sphere of
art; they concerned deleteriously nothing more im-

portant than human life, which such doings helped to keep in its normal condition satisfactorily enough, Smirt supposed, from any divine point of view.

"Yet I would not contemn human life, not wholly," Smirt admitted. "To the aristocracy of Earth—to persons of birth and intelligence and means and culture, and, perhaps above all, to persons with a correct sense of humor—the requirements of civilized living have always seemed both comely and captivating. For these urbane if infrequent persons, living has become, nowadays, a form of art pursued hazardously at the heart of a whirlwind. And living is thus made an ever-dangerous and many-colored and Protean affair for such finely attuned beings as still manage to dissociate themselves from the dull daily labor, the stupidities, the quaint moral ambitions, and the depressing sturdiness, of mankind at large. They get—as the vulgar say—a double kick out of living, nowadays."

For of course (his meditations strolled on) whensoever you considered the human race *en masse*, there were a dreadful number of reputable bourgeois about, all yammering; and, even below the scared bourgeois, you noticed everywhere the unbathed and yelping proletariat. . .Proletarians Smirt took to be the sort of people whose automobiles displayed advertising matter on the cover of the spare tire: and, in academic theory at least, he broad-mindedly ranked them as

135

human beings. . .Well, and all these odd creatures appeared so fretted and so terror-stricken, nowadays, that you mildly wondered at what instant the animals would begin to murder one another.

"It will be an excellent film," Smirt reflected, "with no cuts by the censor. It will be the end of that queer world which the newspapers tell about—and, what is a far graver matter, it will be the temporary end of Earth's urbane aristocracy. My lords, the tumbrils wait: and I fancy these divine drunkards about me know that as well as I do. I condone, therefore, where I cannot exculpate."

After that, Smirt took out of his pocket the forty reis piece which made Smirt omnipotent—within limits,—and he wished for a package of Virginian cigarettes and a box of matches. He inhaled pensively. And Smirt said:

"Against stupidity even the gods are powerless in every handy book of quotations. I begin now to understand that saying. I begin to see that my wit and my fancy and my profundity are at loose ends in a universe which has no real need for these intellectual luxuries."

* *

TWENTY-TWO

ARACHNE RETURNS

*

Now the seven Stewards of Heaven sat at ease, looking over the polished white stone ramparts of their supernal home in the city of Amit, and dealing as they saw fit with the mortal world which was in their keeping. In the while that they drank the dark beer of Sekmet, one after another did they speak the word of power which put upon human beings the needed passions and calamities and desires and weaknesses which would lead these mortals to obey the speaker's will. And Smirt sat with brown Arathron and the six brightly colored children of Arathron observing the handiwork of the Stewards of Heaven.

Smirt could thus see for himself a Danube economic union arranged at Paris, and Austria arrest fleeing Nazi chieftain, and Mrs. B. F. Zogbaum visiting her parents at Galax. He saw Rev. D. W. Cook resign as pastor on account of health, and old Sol on rampage, and mother of 3 slain, mate held. He saw lawyer

137

die in crash as trolley hits truck, and turn of tide indicated by gains in trade. He saw state Solons vote bill to aid wheatgrower, and missing boy found dead in Jersey swimming pool, and he saw people buying Zip razor blades for 39¢ with this coupon, and he saw gayeties galore mark season's height. He saw, in brief, all the sad doings of the Shining Ones as they hammered away at their realism.

Smirt did not like it. He said as much, pointing out that all literate human beings could enjoy at will the delights of romance, if only because the books of the speaker could be borrowed from any public library; he mentioned the address of his publisher; and Smirt added that immortals also might fairly claim a due share of such pleasures.

"There is, for example," Smirt remarked, "the fine legend of Arachne, which I have now in hand—"

"We have heard, often and yet over again," said the Stewards of Heaven, "of a hackney. It is a cross between a cart horse and a race horse. But what, O illustrious Smirt, may be a rackney?"

"Why, do you judge for yourself," replied Smirt.

He spoke the required word of power; and there before them all stood the appearance of that dark young girl who had directed Smirt to the All-Highest.

Then the Shining Ones murmured uneasily. Hagith cried out:

"Beware of the Spider Woman! This is she who devours ignobly the body and the soul also of her victims!"

Smirt replied: "Nonsense! Do I not know a bit better than you do what I create?"

After that, Smirt regarded this not unattractive looking dark girl, for an instant, rather fondly. It appeared permissible in a widower of so many centuries' standing. She was very pretty, very stupid. Smirt thought of six stories into which Arachne might be fitted, but he saw too that no one of his handsome inventions suited her. The nature of this chuckle-headed naïve young creature was at odds with his habitual vein of romantic irony. She had been invented—and that was the trouble—by another creative artist, who for his own ends had made this girl a nicely colored and agreeably shaped moron.

The further trouble was, could anybody, without prejudice, with complete urbanity, describe this happy-hearted and uncommonly pretty Arachne as a moron? She did not know, perhaps, as clearly as Smirt knew, what was the estimated population of Brazil, or the relative specific gravity of hard and soft coal, or the names of the seven stars in the Big Dipper; she might not even know anything about Keats, or about the functions of the pituitary gland, or that Edward Everett had served as the United States' envoy to Great Britain during John Tyler's administration: but she did know how to live serenely and honestly, in contentment with her surroundings. No dreams misled or troubled Arachne. She was, in a dreadful phrase, wholesome.

Oh, but beyond doubt this Arachne had been invented by some botcher who belonged to a most deplorable and quite obsolete school of art. Smirt spoke sharply; and the appearance of the faintly smiling attendant girl was annihilated. Smirt's reproduction of Arachne no longer existed.

Smirt had not planned that destruction consciously. But an odd sense of dismay had possessed him as he regarded the girl's innocent and stupid and so kissable face, because this chit—confound her impudence!—was just the one sort of thing he could never invent. She belonged to a more popular school of art, to an æsthetic kindergarten of sugar and fine sentiments and uncritical optimism. Yet did Smirt desire to be loved foolishly, and above all he wanted to love this young woman very foolishly, without any need to remain urbane. He wanted to share with Arachne, unbothered by the touchstones of experience and savoir faire, and untrammeled by sophistication, all that high and pure and idiotic emotion which, he dimly knew, had been a part of the legend that Smirt could neither remember nor invent. It followed that, for just one instant, the urbanity of Smirt had been flawed with petulance.

But he carried off this error with a light laugh. "I was ill inspired," said Smirt. "Let us destroy and forget the legend of Arachne, for I have thought of a much better story."

* *

TWENTY-THREE

WHAT MEMORY MADE

*

Y es, I have thought of a much better story," Smirt
said, yet again. And thereafter he raided the vast stores
of his scholarship and his erudition with a high hand.

He spoke first the required word of power; and he
spoke also the required Invocation of Memory, saying,
as his instant need was:

"O clement and all-cunning sophist, world-wise
apologist, and learned counsel for the defence of our
foolishness! Friendly apothecary, the compounder of
bland poultices, the chemist of strong healing balms,
for pride's bruises! Skilled brewer of magnanimity;
unerring historian of the false; discreet mortician of
the unpleasant; well-balanced acrobat, not ever to be
tumbled from the trapeze of self-respect! O all-accomplished Memory! do you now give me heed and aid!"

Then Smirt said also: "Let us two conspire together, O wayward lord of all trades, to create again
that world which is governed great-heartedly, by the

fancy of a child; which poets revere as their native
land, hungered after throughout life-long exile; which
is cherished in secret by every common-sense person
bustling about shops and court rooms and office build-
ings; and which by no redeemed spirit in any paradise can be recalled unenviously. O all-accomplished
Memory, give heed! Let our pleasant magic now revive that immortal world which, since it never was,
may not ever perish!"

And after that, with memory to abet him, Smirt
made his implausible, desired world in an eye's
twinkling.

He judged, rightly, that for a divine audience so
prosaic, and virtually illiterate, there was no need to
invent anything new. So out of time-tested materials
he builded his mythic world, after every time-ap-
proved model borrowed from the best fairy tales. For
there was once a princess, Smirt had always remembered, a princess who was more lovely than was any
one of that season's débutantes, and who was more
desirable than a Pulitzer Prize; and with that knowledge firm in his mind, he found it in some sort a sen-
timental pleasure to create a world fit for her in-
habitancy.

So in this world there were magical seas made ready
for Smirt's faintly remembered princess to sail upon,
in a fairy boat drawn by swans; and there were en-

chanted forests, in which she might sleep out a century undisturbed, pending the arrival of some whippersnapper third prince or another; and there was a notable abundance of castles, builded finely of gold or of silver or of copper, suitable for this princess to occupy. There were ogres, and witches, and monsters of every kind, and sorcerers of the most villanous nature, all of them peculiarly easy to kill; and at every cross-roads Smirt stationed a dwarf or a talking fox, or it might be a talking hearth broom, to advise all wayfarers as to what lay ahead in their journeying. And besides that, at fixed intervals of fifteen miles, a king and a queen held their court, setting quaint tests for the valor and the ingenuity of the adoring adventurers who wooed their daughter. She in every instance was a blonde beauty of unexampled perfection; and at each court was established both a good and a bad fairy in regular practice.

Such was the world which Smirt created for the Stewards of Heaven, and which he now exhibited to them, after making antique looking all the contents of this world with a subduing varnish of Celtic glamour. It was a world such as the Shining Ones had not ever imagined during the sad æons they had given over to realism. They beheld now the glories of romance, with an ever-growing enthusiasm which caused all the seven Stewards to remark Bravo! and Encore!

and Author! and Speech! and to make yet other happy observations.

The applauded one received these tributes with his accustomed ease and urbanity; yet all the while, at the bottom of his heart, Smirt was regretting that in no tinseled fairy land such as this could he hope to find the lost legend of Arachne.

*   *

TWENTY-FOUR

ÆSTHETICS OF ARATHRON

*

Arathron spoke, bowing his dark brow; and the ambrosial locks waved from the god's immortal head. (*"For my dream becomes Homeric,"* Smirt *reflected.*) At the feet of Arathron a large mouse-colored goat slumbered peacefully. And thus said the All-Father:

"With no winged words may I praise you fittingly. Appreciation falters before you, O much contriving Smirt, who do not scorn the Stewards of Heaven. Each one of us you have put at ease with some kindly remark. You have been urbane to everybody. You have with unfailing tact concealed that mental superiority of which you could not but be conscious, and you have treated each Shining One as an equal."

Then Smirt of the many books replied to the All-Father, saying:

"Indeed upon their own plane your children entertain me. They compose a leisure class such as I had not previously observed at close range. They live

146

in supreme magnificence, at entire ease, with no need to labor. Yet they do labor, incessantly, and day after day, to upset and to afflict and to destroy mankind, by the hundreds, in time for to-morrow morning's paper. They put upon men every sort of discomfort and suffering, in order to create that queer world which the newspapers tell about. To do that is vile."

"Yet," Arathron interrupted, "yet do you not believe, dear master of all certainty and of all arts, that some such preliminary training in newspaper work may be of benefit to a creative artist by-and-by?"

"I grant," Smirt continued affably, "that the gods are above good and evil, and besides, it seems probable you are false gods who do not exist except in my dream. It is clear that non-existent persons cannot commit crimes, and that in consequence the infamies which you incite cannot exist either. Yes, logic proves that. But logic does not make it equally clear, to any sound logician, why the main interest of the Shining Ones, who upon the whole bore one another, should be invested in human beings?"

Arathron said that he had endeavored to make of each of his children an artist whose medium was human life, and that it had seemed to him a preliminary training in newspaper work—

But all their newspaper work, Smirt interrupted at

once, was bedaubed and degraded by realism. There was in it no touch of the imaginative.

"We perceive that, Smirt, now that you have revealed to us the glories of romance. Yet it had seemed to be our duty to keep life plausible for human beings," replied Arathron, humbly.

Thus he spoke. (*"Hōs phato: for my dream remains Homeric,"* Smirt *reflected.*) And thereafter, even as an iron cauldron is troubled when, surrounded by bright fire, it is melting down the lard of a well-fatted hog; so that at first the large pot bubbles restively, but of a sudden the goodly fat spurts upward on all sides, without any moderation: even so did the urbane patience of Smirt now boil over into candor, in the time that Smirt answered wide-browed Arathron, saying:

"It is far more obviously your duty, my dear sir, to be attending to the conduct of your divine children. Apart from their endless blunders and their wholesale murderings, as when they cause zero weather to creep south or stir up feuds or set fire to department stores or start wars, in their endeavors to enliven the front page of to-morrow morning's paper, they display yet another failing not uncommon among journalists, in that they all drink entirely too much. There is no one of them ever quite sober. What sober

person, to begin with, would think of putting mandrakes and human blood in his beer?"

Arathron looked downward. He stroked the head of
his goat, and he wore now an air of some con-
straint and uneasiness. But Arathron replied only:

"We drink the dark beer of Sekmet, Smirt, so that
we may forget our divine destiny. There is but one
doom for the super-eminent, whether he be a true
god or a false god; and none may escape it."

"And what, Arathron, is that doom?"

"It is revealed to the super-eminent alone, Smirt—"

"Well, but, upon my word—!" said Smirt.

"—And at no time," Arathron continued, "is the
thinking of any divine person, whether he be a true
god or a false god, quite free from deliberating that
doom which awaits him at the appointed hour. Moreover, we drink the dark beer of Sekmet so that we
Shining Ones may forget those insane beings who are
above us upon this mountain top."

"Let us not speak of the public at large, Arathron,
for I have seen them. It is a sad truth that the gods
also must depend upon the patronage and the continued good will of the public at large."

Thus he spoke. (*"For we stay Homeric," thought
Smirt.*) But even as a questing lion is made glad when
he perceives from afar the wide-horned bull, or it
may be a stiff-shanked sheep very rich in fat; and in

his deep mind he already devours the sweet flesh; so that he advances boldly into the pasture, without any dread of the fleet dogs or the sharp spears of the herdsman: even so did the All-Father Arathron at this season put aside each baneful thought which had troubled his renowned nature, causing his godlike spirit to tremble within him like an emotional blanc mange; and he spoke afterward, with the well-famed merriment of grigs and of marriage bells, saying:

"What do these lesser worries matter, now that we have managed to get in touch with your publisher, and have been allowed his usual discount to divine customers?"

"You surprise me," Smirt answered the All-Father, "for that tall being is not at all the person to go a-whoring after strange gods. As in public he above his confrères, so in private do his principles tower above reproach; and indeed in every respect I find the man to be as incomprehensible as are his royalty reports."

"Yet do you see for yourself, dear Master!"

And Arathron waved a thin dark hand in the direction of Arathron's offspring.

*　　*

TWENTY-FIVE

RESULT OF MUCH READING

*

Smirt saw that to every side of him the children of Arathron sat quietly reading. They had put aside for the while their newspaper work and all stupid realistic dealings with men and women. They merely read: and they paused only to drink silently the dark beer of Sekmet which kept the Shining Ones perpetually fuddled. There were signs up everywhere which said Silence.

Now and then one of the engrossed Stewards would put aside his book, and he would tiptoe over to an unabridged dictionary in twelve volumes, and he would look up the meaning of a word; after that, he would return happily to his reading. And now and then, too, they spoke in subdued whispers, as the Stewards conferred together.

"Never had I hoped to find," said Och, "a genius who depicts with such utter loveliness, such impish wit, and such tender humanity, man's endless searching after the golden dream which he creates for himself."

Bethor replied, "Anyone with a soul to appreciate beauty will find in countless pages of these books that which no other living writer can offer."

It was then Phaleg leaned back in his chair. He cupped his chin with his right hand; afterward this handsome red-colored giant rubbed the palm of his right hand against the palm of his left hand, meditatively, and he pursed up his lips.

"These books," said Phaleg, "are very deep. One needs quite a knowledge of world literature and mythology to understand them."

"They strike," agreed Hagith, "a responsive chord in the hearts of every type of reader."

It was in this way that the Stewards of Heaven were each reading the books of Smirt. Each one of them had a complete set in the definitive edition. And when each Steward had read through his set from the first volume to the last volume, then the Shining Ones arose, crying:

"Homage to Smirt! At last his genius has been recognized fittingly. Henceforward let his æsthetic theories prevail throughout the planet which is in our keeping. Hail to thee, Smirt! not in vain have we read your books very reverently. Hereafter shall all human life become as you have decreed."

And Smirt, looking over the ramparts of Àmit, perceived they spoke truthfully. The planet beneath Smirt had been disinfected of all matter suited to newspaper publication. The planet had been made colorful with all magics. Everywhither rode abridged likenesses of Smirt upon magnificent quests; and each one of these secondary Smirts was speaking the most polished diction, and was doing urbanely any number of impossible things in the lands beyond common-sense.

"Come now," said Smirt, "but this is most gratifying, for it is in the lands beyond common-sense, if anywhere, that I must look for the legend of Arachne."

PART FIVE

ABOUT A CHANGED PLANET

*   *

*

"*Xenophon consecrated fifty courtesans to the Corinthian Venus, in pursuance of the vow which he had made when he besought the goddess to give him victory in the Olympian games; and the text of a remarkable legend of the Creation, acquired by the late Mr. A. H. Rhind in 1861, from a tomb on the left bank of the Nile at Thebes, is yet preserved in the British Museum, where it bears the number 10,188.*"

* *

TWENTY-SIX

AIREL OF THE BROWN HAIR

*

Smirt travelled happily in a reorganized planet, seeking after the legend of Arachne. He had got, at all events, into some legend or another legend, now that a charmed staff guided him. This staff, he reflected, had been cut from the Tree of Knowledge, when the Cross of the Saviour of the Protestant Episcopal Church likewise was a portion of that green, many-branching tree in the midst of Eden: and in consequence Smirt carried this staff in his right hand, knowing that if at any time he laid down the staff he would at once regain his sophistication and quite lose his way in this legend.

He toiled thus through a ravine overgrown with brambles, with flowering gorse, with blackberry bushes, and with small, very tough vines which vexatiously entangled his legs, and which caught about his ankles, like strong wires. He came to an open field in which lay the dead body of a young man extremely like Smirt, wrapped and confined everywhere with the weavings of some great spider, so that this partially devoured body resembled a large gray cocoon. Smirt found this curious; and more curious still seemed the fact that a half-finished poem was clutched in the right hand of the half-finished corpse. However, it was not a specially good poem.

And after that, Smirt went by a black sign post, which said, in a lemon yellow lettering:

"You are now leaving Legend of Iannak. Come again. Legend of Airel begins 500 feet ahead. Beware of soft shoulders."

Then Smirt passed toward a white mountain and a black mountain: and as he approached them yet another curious sight was before Smirt, for these mountains hurled themselves upon each other with a violence so great that both mountains were shattered into fragments. Smirt paused, a little perturbed: for everywhere in front of him the air was now thick with a hailing of black stones and of white stones, as though crows and white pigeons were fighting together.

Through this two-colored hailing came a brown-haired woman walking mournfully, in leggings of deerskin. She had upon her head a three-pointed crown of gold; and a big brooch of gold glittered on her right shoulder, holding about her a cloak of two colors, a cloak of scarlet and of a green like the green of young ferns. Such was Airel the conversation woman.

"You have done me a great wrong," said Airel the conversation woman, "for these mountains were my entire estate. And I lived handsomely there, in a tower of glass, with my blue and yellow birds to attend me, and with my blue cow whose milk never failed, and with my four whispers which brought to me conversation from every quarter of the lands beyond common-sense."

Smirt said to her, "That is a good way to be living, Airel of the Brown Hair, having your command over these fine things."

"But it is not the way I am any longer, Smirt of the high misdeeds, now that my blue cow and my tower of glass are in flinders, and my birds have flown away, and my whispers have fallen into deep silence, because of that ruining staff of yours."

Then Smirt answered her fondly: "To hear that is a grief which I cannot put any bounds to, O queen of this world's women. Yet it seemed to me that your two mountains fought of their own accord, without my having incited them in the least."

"Be that as it may be, Smirt, it was your coming which has destroyed all my belongings, leaving me, O my grief, without any fortune in this kingdom."

"It was unintentional, I can but repeat, O beautiful

159

kind woman. And I would willingly make any amends within my power; but to restore mountains is not in my power, nor can I put fresh milk and lowing back into a dead cow."

"At the very least, Smirt," said the conversation woman, "and in mere justice, Smirt, you ought now to provide me with a son to be the support of my penniless old age."

"In fact, to a sound logician that appears more reasonable," Smirt admitted; "and I do not know but that it might be a pleasure, too, to a widower of so many centuries' standing."

"Yet it is not reason I am asking of you, O tall comely hero, no, nor pleasure either, but mere justice."

"Then let justice be done," said Smirt, "for I am lord of the high, the low and the middle justice. As such, I would recommend a *habeas corpus*."

Thus speaking, he affably went up into the gold and silver bed of Airel.

*   *

TWENTY-SEVEN

AFFAIRS OF THE FAMILY

*

So did Smirt enter into the gold and silver bed of
Airel the conversation woman, between the bright
curtains which had the color of larkspur and were
hung upon rods of copper: and Airel went with him.
It was not sleep that they looked for in this bed. And
a good fortune blessed their endeavors without any
remarkable delay, for before morning the labor pains
came upon Airel, and she was delivered of her desired
son.

"You lose no time," said Smirt, as he laid the child
in its bronze cradle. Even as he spoke a wind blew
out of the dawn, and the child was whisked away like
a pink bit of paper. "Thus quickly do our blessings
vanish," Smirt moralized.

But Airel replied: "I do not like pessimism. It is
written, O man of the house, that joy cometh in the
morning."

Then as they sat down to their breakfast, of elk's

meat and honey and oatmeal, and when Airel had poured ale into amber cups, a young man approached them; and he said fondly to Airel the conversation woman,—

"Joy cometh in the morning."

"Joy of my life," said Airel, "it is great wisdom you are speaking."

After that, the young hero looked at Smirt, without any fondness, but the grave brown eyes which regarded Smirt were compassionate. The young champion was tall and comely, having a green cloak about him; about his curled dark hair was a red chaplet of sweet-smelling rowan berries; and his face was the face of Smirt.

"But who, pray, is this whippersnapper?" Smirt asked of Airel.

She replied, "It is my son Elair, he who was born this morning to be the mainstay of my old age."

"But certainly you lose no time," said Smirt.

"It is time's part to lose us," said Airel, gravely.

And Smirt answered her: "In any case, you have not as yet any old age for him to be the mainstay of. So do let us all three sit down to breakfast without any more apothegms, or any more argument either, Airel of the Brown Hair."

"My grief!" said Airel, keening, "there is anger in my very heart! It is not right of you, O Smirt of the high misdeeds, to be denying me my old age whenever I want it."

"Joy of my life," said the young man Elair, to his mother Airel, "it is great wisdom you are speaking."

Then the young man Elair took up a pipe of seven reeds. He played upon it: and as he played, old age came upon Airel, and upon Elair likewise, until both of them were shrivelled and thin beings, as white as the foaming of waves in moonshine, and the wind carried them away very lightly, leaving Smirt alone at the breakfast table.

"Regret has come into my heart," said Smirt, "now that life has gone out of Airel. I lament Airel, the delight of my eyes, she who was comely and generous and pursuing. I am sorrowful now that my son Elair is blown away by the west wind. I am not happy in this place. My courage is fallen down; my heart is a wet sponge filled with bitter tears.

"It would be well for Smirt could I follow my age-stricken family down the long ways of the wind, now that my very old family has gone away in a fume and a dudgeon, or it might be in a huff. My hearthstone and my breakfast are cold: my urbanity fails me when I look at their coldness. I lament Airel of the Brown Hair, who can re-warm neither.

"There was no coldness in her many-colored bed. She was fair and nimble. It was pleasant to put birth upon her in six conversations. My thinking follows after Airel the conversation woman in a gray weeping mist; my grief follows my son Elair. I would like to have seen more of him. It is a pity the way I am, now that the west wind has broken up my home life.

"Yet, after all," said Smirt, "after all, this young woman was not Arachne. No; I have wandered into the wrong legend; and my quest, as yet, remains unfulfilled."

* *

TWENTY-EIGHT

INTRODUCES AN ANGEL

*

Smirt journeyed on, with the staff guiding him, into a Druid wood. In this wood he met with the more brilliantly colored birds and animals of all latitudes and with five monsters such as are indigenous to the lands beyond common-sense, so that every step of Smirt's way was of never failing interest.

He met also with an armed fighting-man, and this Kilian of the Red Marsh defied Smirt to single combat. Inasmuch as Smirt's staff had now been turned into a sword, this appeared reasonable. So the two men fought with heroic valor, without either of them injuring the other. Then a fleecy cloud hovered over their combat and, oozing downward between the two champions, pushed them apart. An angel stepped out from the rosy depths of this cloud and inquired reprovingly:

"Wherefore do you fight, the one child of Heaven against another? I call upon you to be reconciled and to become as brothers. Be of one heart and of one mind, and turn your forces against the enemies of true religion. That is my advice to you to-day, as it was my advice yesterday to another pair of game-cocks, to the Sieurs Oliver and Roland."

Thus speaking, the angel waved a palm branch over each of the two champions, to denote that the honors of their interrupted duel were evenly divided, and the angel vanished. Kilian of the Red Marsh agreed with Smirt that the angel had spoken sensibly, in all points except one. They could not become as brothers, Kilian considered, until one of them had married the other's sister.

"But I have no sister," said Smirt.

"That does not matter," Kilian replied, "for I have a sister, whose good looks are equalled only by her piety. It is true she was carried away by Crogan Kno-bald, the Dwarf King, and that she married him last year."

"Yet is it well, my dear Kilian, to come between husband and wife?"

"But is it seemly, Smirt, to be contradicting an angel? You forget that my sister is noted for her piety."

"Oh, well, of course, if you put it that way!" said Smirt. "Moreover, you mentioned her good looks also. And besides, it may be that your sister, in addition to her good looks, has also the good fortune to be called Arachne?"

Kilian was frankly puzzled. "But how, Smirt, could she be called anything of that sort?"

"Why, one has sponsors," Smirt explained. "And they come forward, either immediately after the Second Lesson at Morning or Evening Prayer, or at such other time as the Minister shall appoint—"

But Kilian stayed unconvinced. "Be that as it may be, Smirt, my sister is called Oriana; and I have never heard her called anything else."

"Then I am still in the wrong legend," said Smirt. "But that, after all, is no reason for flying in the face of an angel."

They gave over their talking for that while, and they went through a patch of fir-trees, to an iron door with gold writing on it. They beat in the door. They came thus to a rose garden where it was always June, because the garden was fenced with a golden thread, such as used to defend the palaces of the Æsir in the older time, and this thread prevented the entrance of any other month. They could not break this thread, they found, but they stooped and crawled under it without any special difficulty, because they were not months.

When the Dwarf King came out angrily against these trespassers, he came in gold armor, with a bright carbuncle in his helmet; and his delight to see his brother-in-law was unbounded. "Kilian of my heart, my pulse and my treasure," Crogan declared, in a thin and high-pitched voice, "there is nobody I would be embracing more willingly."

"Health and good days!" cried out Kilian, hugging the doomed monarch with compassion.

Then Crogan embraced Smirt also, saying, "Health and long life, O friend's friend!"

"The pleasure," Smirt replied, "is inexpressible. And I desire for you, sir, as long a life as piety may permit."

* *

TWENTY-NINE

OF PIETY AND ORIANA

*

After that, the three men went together into the underground home of Crogan Knobald. A soft twilight reigned in the vast hall of the palace. The walls were of polished marble, inlaid with obscene designs in gold and silver, for Crogan was not of the true religion. The floor of this hall was formed of a single agate, so far as Smirt could make out; the ceiling was of sapphire; and from this ceiling hung shining rubies, like so many red stars in the blue sky of a spring evening.

There was nowhere any palace more remarkable than was this palace, which, as Crogan Knobald explained, the Dwarf King had inherited, along with his rose garden, from his great-great-grandfather, King Laurin of Gargazon. The palace did, however, need to be equipped with a more modern lighting system, Smirt reflected, in the same instant Smirt perceived he was wholly wrong.

For all at once the entire place became brilliant as an August morning, now that Oriana had entered. Her girdle and necklace were jeweled with thirty-nine gems, and in her coronet was a diamond, the third largest of all diamonds known in the lands beyond common-sense; and this diamond shone like the sun, bringing the brightness of day whithersoever it came. But Oriana was far more beautiful than any one of these things, with a sedate and a saintlike loveliness. No man could take his eyes from the quiet and radiant and holy face of Oriana; nor did Smirt make any such hopeless attempt.

When Crogan went to fetch wine, then Smirt complimented the lady, with his customary ease and elegance, upon her fine fortune in being able to rule in this wonderful palace as its queen.

She replied in unaffected sincerity that, although she would never forget the home and the friends of her girlhood, no woman could be more fortunate than was Oriana in her present estate. Crogan was always good and kind, and she had learned to esteem the countless virtues of her dear husband, upon an uncarnal plane, because Crogan Knobald was not so sensually disposed and obsessed as were most other men. There was in his love no grossness and no crude materialism, this dove-like and saintly queen told them, on account of a providential accident in his youth.

"He was injured just here," she explained to Smirt. Smirt replied, "Ouch!"

"It has followed," Oriana continued, "that, while this remains, he is burdened with neither of these; and our affection is thus kept perfect and holy."

Then Kilian told of the angel's command, and Oriana began to look at Smirt more and more thoughtfully. In her gray-colored, very large eyes he perceived unshed tears. She bent toward him, she laid her hand in Smirt's lap, saying sorrowfully:

"My friend, what choice have I in this matter? The ways of Heaven are beyond our conjecture and beyond our disputing, equally. Yet you, I observe, have not ever been chastened by any accident: your love will be gross and material, I fear. It will trouble me vigorously. Oh, but at each instant I become more certain of that fact."

"Divine Oriana," Smirt replied sympathetically, patting her hand, "in this world we must all bear our crosses."

"In this world," said Kilian, "there is nothing like inspecting the property before one signs a lease. You are both prudent and virtuous, my sister."

"I do not understand what you are talking about, Kilian; but yours, Smirt, is a pious reflection." And it was plain, now that Oriana had withdrawn her hand pensively from under Smirt's half detaining hand, that Oriana had found comfort in Smirt's axiom. "Yes, we must all bear our crosses, howsoever enormous, for the will of Heaven must not be disputed. I will put poison in Crogan's wine," said Oriana, and she proceeded to do so.

The Dwarf King died quickly, in considerable astonishment, you could see, but without any apparent pain.

Then Smirt made ready to take Oriana as his wife, and Kilian sat down beside them, smilingly anticipative, now that the angel's command was about to be obeyed in every particular. But hardly had the three of them prepared with all suitable fervor to observe these religious duties when the two brothers of Crogan Knobald came into the underground palace.

They were impious heathen persons, who did not respect angels. Instead they came, bearing willow wands, with dark anger in their hearts; and they cast Druid spells sacrilegiously, in the while that they upset the plainly expressed will of Heaven.

So was Kilian transformed into a green toad, and Oriana into a dove-colored snake, which at once swallowed the green toad. But upon Smirt the depraved brothers of Crogan Knobald laid the Curse of Two Fortnights.

*　　*

THIRTY

CITY OF THE DEAD

*

Now the wits of Smirt were put away from Smirt's keeping by the Curse of Two Fortnights. He who had sat among the gods, now wandered in a lonely savageness, dribbling at the mouth which no longer conversed affably. Instead, Smirt moaned and whimpered like a hurt dog; and Smirt lived in the wilder lands beyond common-sense as a beast lives, nakedly, searching after roots and grubs, and then leaving them untasted, because upon no occasion during his dream did Smirt eat any food.

He made his lair in a stone city, upon which its special doom had fallen, in the older times, turning all to stone. The olive-trees and the palm-trees of this city were of stone; in the quiet streets and bazaars, and in the houses of this city, you found men and women and children of various sizes, all eternally poised in whatsoever trivial or commonplace action they were engrossed by when, without any warning, its doom fell upon this city, and changed all its people into bluish-gray stone statues, in the midst of their shopping and love-making and stolid talking. Thus had a remarkably beautiful girl, of eighteen or thereabouts, been left forever straining at the stool in an outhouse; and one middle-aged citizen had been petrified while he was shaving. For another queer thing, there were in this city four large spider webs, the largest which Smirt had ever seen, and in each of them dangled the skeleton of a young man picked clean of flesh.

Here Smirt fared very lonelily, seeing no human creature. In his clouded mind there was panic, and remorse troubled him also, but he could not divine for what reason; nor did Smirt think urbane thoughts under the Curse of Two Fortnights.

He thought always of the dead persons whom he had known, and of how little their lives had mattered. All these persons had passed away, fritteringly, giving over one moment after another moment to kindly and laborious and trivial doings, until no more moments remained. They had made nothing; they had achieved nothing; and nothing survived of them except a few torn and scattered memories in Smirt's clouded mind.

For his mind was all clouds, it seemed to him, gray clouds which moved continuously, and which boiled over one another, very lazily, and which opened now and then with pale vistas in which you saw faintly the faces of the dead whom you had known when these faces had color and movement in them. And yet his mind was a ticking also, the ticking of a black onyx clock which he had seen and had heard ticking in some happier place, he did not remember where; and this ticking counted relentlessly every moment of Smirt's living, telling you there was one instant, then another instant, and then yet another, but only one instant at a time, and telling you that no one of these instants could ever return.

And besides that, his mind was a thin buzzing and a futile blustering, like the noise which is made by a blue-bottle fly; so that this restive little noise was combined with a not ever resting ticking, in a mixture which troubled Smirt a great deal as he wandered about the dead city of Ras Sem. It was not cheering to observe its petrified citizens forever arrested in the midst of their kindly and laborious and trivial doings. And to consider them quite urbanely proved a difficult matter.

For you could not think properly with a cloudiness and a ticking and a buzzing. These were not the instruments, Smirt reflected, with which people made urbane thoughts. And he knew very well what he needed.

* *

THIRTY-ONE

WHICH BECOMES LOGICAL

*

What I need, what I really need, to think with,"
Smirt said, in strict confidence, to a black dog—
which was not utterly black, however, because it had
a white muzzle and a white tail and four white feet
also—"is a brain."

"That is true," replied the black dog. "And it
ought to weigh not less than forty-two ounces, of
which the gray substance should represent about
thirty-eight per cent. of the entire weight. I must tell
you this, Smirt, because now that you have lost your
wits they have been foisted upon me, of all luckless
creatures."

"I rather liked having my wits," said Smirt, wist-
fully.

"But I do not like having your wits," said the black
dog. "I detest them cordially. They are forcing me at
this very instant to tell you that your main trouble is
aphasia. You forget things."

176

"I cannot concede that, black dog, for I do not remember anything I have forgotten."

"You forget, for example," said the unhappy black dog—who was now being compelled, willy-nilly, to use Smirt's intelligence just as Smirt had formerly used it—"that the Gallitzin Tunnel through the Alleghany Mountains, eleven miles west of Altoona, Pennsylvania, is only 3600 feet long."

"In fact," said Smirt, with some show of interest, "why should any human life be longer than a tunnel? I had not thought of the matter in that light. But, now my own wits have pointed it out, I can see that if my life were just 3600 feet long I would be in a sad taking."

Then the black dog began to smile in a way which, somehow, appeared equivocal, and he wagged his white tail with contentment.

"Moreover, Smirt," said the black dog, "you forget that the metal chromium was discovered and isolated by Vauquelin in 1797."

"Whereas I am not isolated at all!" said Smirt, brightening still more. "I have never been isolated. So that I am far luckier than chromium, or than beryllium either, upon which Vauquelin played the same trick during the following year."

"Finally, Smirt, you forget that the chief interest of North Dakota is agriculture, which produces in that state every cereal and other crop known to the north temperate zone."

"Whereas I am not the least bit interested in agriculture!" Smirt declared happily. "I never have been. Nor do I have to live in North Dakota, where, as I now recall, black dog, nine and six-tenths less fortunate people do have to live to every square mile. I would find it quite intolerable to have to associate every day with six-tenths of a person. And all this, just as you say, I am spared. Well, well, but there is nothing like logic: and it does pay, in the long run, to reason these things out to the bottom with one's own wits."

"So now you see for yourself," said the black dog. "Your wits have returned to you, and I am very well rid of them. But you, you will need all those precious wits of yours before the Spider Woman has done with Smirt."

Then he went away, laughing unpleasantly, in a way which Smirt did not think respectful, somehow, although that was hardly the immediate point.

"The immediate point is, he is not a real dog. He has inside him no traditional love for mankind, but only bits of string. Moreover, his back lifts off. So of course he has to go back to the radiator in my writing room," Smirt reasoned it out. "It would be wholly absurd to expect any such black wooden dog to remain here talking with me, because no species of dog can talk."

For now that Smirt had considered logically his good luck along with his bad luck, the Curse of Two Fortnights was lifted; and along with his lost wits all Smirt's urbanity had returned to him. He took out of his pocket the forty reis piece, and procured a fresh package of cigarettes, with the necessary matches, and he passed jauntily from the dead city of Ras Sem into the highest circles of philosophy.

＊　　＊

THIRTY-TWO

IN THE PAPER PALACE

＊

Now that his wits were restored to him, and he was
once more a sound logician, Smirt went, rather as a
matter of course, into the palace of Rani. The home
of the South Wind's third daughter was builded handsomely, out of the very best quality of paper; by a
great triumph of engineering, it was balanced upon
a gilt weather-cock, in order that its inhabitants might
not ever fall into set ways, or any paralyzing routine
of life; and into this variable, high palace the charms
of the South Wind's third daughter had uplifted the
finest of existent minds, so that in this place her servitors could observe and criticize the doings of time and
chance without any bias.

Nor was that everything: for the servants of Rani
played in wide fields of thought. Hour in, and hour
out, did her followers speak to one another, and to
nobody else. And it was about every sociological matter which entered into the doings of time and chance

that they spoke to one another, hour in, and hour out, after a sublime fashion which time and chance would no doubt have found informative; and inasmuch as none of these philosophers had ever for one instant listened to his fellows, all passed happily enough in the paper palace of Rani.

"One perceives," said Smirt, "that the humanities are well honored hereabouts, and that these are not ordinary philosophers."

A doctor of laws replied: "These, Smirt, are the wise followers of Rani. They think each man his own sociological thoughts, and they voice these thoughts without ever ceasing, who know that for such fine minds the universe and its contents are toys to be played with."

"Well, but," said Smirt, "this savors of *hubris*, of that overweening pride which destroyed Œdipus, and Prometheus, and so many other protagonists of Greek drama. Let us avoid *hubris*. Let us remember, gentlemen, that in point of fact it is the Stewards of Heaven who play with this special part of the universe and with all its contents, including philosophers."

"That, Smirt, is but a gross and material consideration," returned a lexicographer.

"You remind me, sir, of my late fiancée Oriana—"

"I remind you rather that such gods, if there be any

gods, have their divine will with our bodies; but all we live snug and secure from such foolishness, each man abiding in the inmost nook of his own brain cells, thinking our sociological thoughts, and deriding the gods, who have no power over our minds."

Up went the eyebrows of Smirt, and his shoulders also went up, shruggingly; but his doubtfulness stayed unspoken. He remarked, instead:

"You reason adroitly. Yet has this continuous thinking at any time revealed to you gentlemen why on earth the All-Highest ever created mankind? For that one sociological problem does baffle me, I admit. I cannot quite believe it was done solely for the diversion of Smirt—"

"The possible intentions of his just not impossible Creator," replied a grammarian, "is an affair with which man has no concern. Man exists endowed with certain qualities. To develop, and to make full use of, these qualities, in so far as stays convenient under the local police regulations, is his proper sociological course. It is a course which, in plain reason, could not anger any rational Creator under Whose direct supervision the hornet stings, the hawk murders, and the polecat is unpopular."

Then a pantologist said: "All human freedom consists in the affirmation of the inevitable. Thus alone may one achieve *teshuvah*, the identification of one's will with the will of the All-Highest. Yet have not many psychologists equated this self-negation with a lack of self-esteem as a fairly constant element in the neuroses of an Hebraic windbag? That is a weighty point; that is fundamental stuff such as Ludwig Lewisohn publishes; and people admire it."

"Moreover, in considering the All-Highest, and eschatology in general," said a bachelor of science, "one must distinguish between the rude fables of antiquity and the refinements of polite religion. For I am meditating, this afternoon, upon the sociology of Doomsday. The dead will then arise, we are informed, unchanged. I infer that all the blessed will arise with their bowels, which will undoubtedly continue to function. In Our Father's house are many outhouses. Yes, there will be comfort stations in Paradise, with millions of rest rooms; and it is a solemn thought to reflect upon the holy persons enthroned in them every morning."

"But each one of you," said Smirt, "strays from the point, like a broken compass. I have asked a plain question, a question of some importance. And each one of you three has veered away from it, to reverberate another question."

"How does it matter, Smirt?" asked Rani, who was the lovely and erratic queen over all these philosophers. "Is it not better to be broad-minded?"

"Well, now that all depends," said Smirt. "There are far too many minds which broaden by the simple process of becoming more shallow. Yet in most circumstances it is well to be broad-minded; for otherwise, there is no telling."

The South Wind's daughter regarded him pensively; and pensively she began, you could see, to approve of her newest philosopher.

Rani was clothed, to a certain extent at least, in a fine robe of transparent iridescent stuff, colored like the wings of a blue-bottle fly; and this was embroidered with very small scarlet fig-leaves. Her golden head-dress had the quaint shaping of a coiled serpent with its head raised.

Rani remarked, after a moment of appraising reflection:

"And besides, Smirt, if you and I were human, it might be we would need to trouble over these human problems. But as matters stand, they do not concern us, any more than we need to know why a dog must turn about in a circle before he lies down or why moths fly toward a lighted candle and destroy themselves joyfully."

"Yet I do know, Rani, about the King of Hearts and about barbers' poles also—"

"For the rest," said Rani, standing a-tiptoe to pat his cheek, "you are Smirt the Peripatetic Episcopalian, and I am the South Wind's own daughter. Let us be content with our high stations."

"Revered Rani, it is in a dream that we occupy these stations. And that makes a difference, it may be," said Smirt, dubiously. "However, even in a dream it is pleasant to become a philosopher and to lead a contemplative life in this handsome palace of yours. Yes, it is quite gratifying to have so many superb minds forever at work to the right and the left of you, and to hear them delivering such valuable opinions about every topic unceasingly. It is still more gratifying—I need hardly say—to be cherished by a creature so lovable and so wholly lovely as you are, dear lady."

"Ah, but," said Rani, "the best is yet to be."

And at that, Smirt shook his head, forebodingly.

* *

THIRTY-THREE

THE PHILOSOPHY OF RANI

*

Yes, dreaming was pleasant enough, Smirt reflected, in the good graces of Rani. None the less was it necessary to be firm when Rani talked about marriage and, a very little later, about dispensing with marriage.

"These are suggestions which pain me," Smirt told her. "It is true that your family owes me a wife, O daughter of the South Wind, but I have no need of a wife now that I have turned philosopher. No, there is Socrates who, being dead, yet speaketh, dehorting the philosophic from matrimony. No, these suggestions are the sort of thing which one expects from mortal women, and from goddesses also, but you, my adored Rani, are the supreme passion of my life, at this special instant; and I do not propose to have the supreme passion of my life destroyed by any such antics."

"On the other hand—" said Rani.

"Do you consider, O heart's dearest," Smirt

186

pleaded, as he sat down beside Rani, on her double bed, in order to reason more comfortably, "do you consider the grotesque indignity of the performance you contemplate! In no variant does it admit an element of gracefulness. It betrays one into a frame of mind which is neither tactful nor urbane. Indeed, it temporarily remits the intelligence; and to do that is not good for a philosopher. Moreover, this performance results in sweat, in spasms, in slime, and in smells. It results, in brief, in the instant need of a bath. Yet it is in this horrible way that every woman expects a man to express his affection!"

"Nevertheless—" said Rani.

"I can but suggest," said Smirt, "that relatively few women possess any imagination. They resent, it may be, the male's larger gift of imagination, which attains its most epic proportions when the man is in love. They beguile him therefore into the inconsequent notion that his imaginings have something to do with a conjuncture of sewer pipes. They suggest to him that the most undignified goings-on, in a bed such as we now occupy, are the goal and the logical result of all his lofty imaginings. In this way do women manage to discredit the imagination of every man, sooner or later. And in this way also do women find for all abstract notions a common denominator, so that the justice of Airel, the piety of Oriana, and the philosophy of Rani become indistinguishable the one from another."

"Still—" said Rani.

"I present this theory," said Smirt, "simply as an hypothesis. A learned author has remarked that no man quite understands women; and he might well have added that in this respect women are far from unique, inasmuch as no man can quite understand anything. I cannot understand, for example, why you do not keep your hands to yourself. I understand only that illusions are highly entertaining to Smirt. I must in consequence cherish my illusions; and you, O my dearest Rani, are the chief of my illusions, at of course this special stage in my dream."

"Yet—" said Rani.

"I can but entreat you," said Smirt, "not to persuade, reason, moralize, dispute, wrangle, and bandy arguments, with such torrents of eloquence; for my mind is made up. Yes, dear lady, it is quite pretty; but then I have seen a great many of them, you know."

"But—" said Rani.

"No, my darling," said Smirt. "In the palace of Rani my pursuits shall be purely intellectual. Even in the bed of Rani I intend to remain upright and unadventurous. Meanwhile, if you insist on it, I do not mind kissing you in a purely philosophic way."

Rani said nothing.

But Smirt said, almost immediately: "Did I not stipulate 'in a purely philosophic way'? Ah, well, but Epicurus also was a philosopher; and there is certainly something to be said for the hedonistic school."

In his heart, however, Smirt was reflecting: "After all, this young woman is not Arachne. No; I am still in the wrong legend; and my quest, as yet, remains unfulfilled."

* *

THIRTY-FOUR

IS PAST IN A JIFFY

*

Smirt left the bed of Rani and the delights of her paper palace without further delay. He quitted them in a jiffy (which he preferred upon the whole to a trice, although neither of them was in appearance quite what Smirt had expected) because Smirt's honor was engaged in the quest of Arachne's legend, and because the trivial pretty face of Arachne stayed always in Smirt's thinking. He had promised, by no less than seven revered matters, to restore to this girl her lost estate in the lands beyond common-sense. It was a fact which debarred shilly-shallying. He must keep his promise, he deduced, with the unhesitancy of a sound logician, in a jiffy.

But in a jiffy he found that her legend was not known at Camelot: no one of Arthur's knights, and not even gray Merlin Ambrosius, could direct Smirt to that lost estate. Charlemagne and the twelve paladins who were then in attendance upon Charle-

magne had heard no report of Arachne, nor had bland
Bishop Turpin heard of her either. At Tara of the
Kings, Fionn Mac Uail shook his wise head regretfully; no, he had known many women, but never
Arachne: at Tara, not even Diarmuid, whom all
women cherished because of his love spot, had been
pursued by Arachne, in so far as Diarmuid could remember. And at Bagdad it was the same disappoint-
ing story: Haroun Alraschid was sympathetic, even
cordial; if Smirt wanted a woman, here were three
dozen young virgins, each one of them more fair
than the moon, at Smirt's disposal: but of these un-
pierced pearls, of these most lovely fillies not as yet
tamed by any rider (so Mesrour the head eunuch reported) no one was Arachne. Nor when Smirt came
to the court of Prester John in a jiffy could the king-
bishop or any of the seventy-two emperors who served
Prester John, after they had consulted together, in a
large hall hung with red panther skins, help Smirt in
Smirt's questing.

Then, still in a jiffy, Smirt went about the kingdom of El Dorado, where the reigning monarch was
oiled every morning and sprinkled all over with gold
dust. And afterward Smirt visited the Hyperboreans,
on the other side of the North Star. And in neither
country could Smirt find the legend of Arachne.

Then at Atlantis Smirt consulted, without any least

success, the supreme oracle of Poseidon, in a circular temple builded of ivory and of silver, and capped with tall pinnacles of gold and orichalc. Through four of the Fortunate Islands likewise did Smirt seek after Arachne's legend without finding any trace of it. And Smirt travelled among more barbarous peoples too, among men that had the heads and the soft pendant ears of setter dogs, and among men who were shaped like eels, and among men who were so oddly constructed as to possess, each one of them in his own person, the organs proper to both sexes. And among none of these peoples could Smirt find the legend of Arachne.

After that, Smirt questioned the Samoyeds, another remarkably hirsute nation, whose faces were upside down, and who shed their skins once a year. And Smirt questioned the Umeloi, the Hill-Dwellers, a black people with flaming red eyes and very bright yellow hair, who lived in elm-trees, in large egg-shaped nests made out of gaily colored bird feathers. And Smirt questioned also the terrible army of Gog and Magog, where they lay encamped in the Caucasus Mountains, waiting until the hour came for them to destroy all this world and to ravage the golden city of Jehovah.

But everywhere Smirt questioned in vain. No one of these peoples had the desired legend, and no learned person with whom Smirt talked in the lands beyond common-sense could tell Smirt anything about the Arachne whose trivial pretty face stayed so obstinately in Smirt's thinking.

"It is needful," said Smirt, "that something should be done at once about this unsatisfactory state of affairs."

*   *

THIRTY-FIVE

THE WAY OF A MAID

*

Now the appearance of Arachne haunted Smirt, saying: "You have talked, and strutted, and talked,—and then you have talked some more. But you have not ever found my legend, you have not restored to me any of my lost estate in these lands beyond common-sense, as you most faithfully promised you would do, when you swore a great oath by those curious gods of yours."

"That is true, Arachne. . .And for the rest, as a matter of course I have talked. One has to keep up the conversation. But I most certainly have not strutted. My modesty is proverbial."

Then the appearance of Arachne would smile somewhat. "It does not matter," she said, cryptically. "I rather like it."

"In fact, Arachne, now that you have brought up the topic, modesty is a rare virtue."

"And it seems particularly praiseworthy, Smirt, in

194

any Virginian gentleman who has so little to be modest about, does it not?"

"Come now, Arachne, but that also is true! You have a logical mind, my dear—"

She had colored up deliciously. But she frowned also, saying,—

"To begin with—"

"I know," said Smirt. "But I do not apologize, because you really are my dear, at all events during this special stage of my dream. And in any case, I was only going on to observe that my virtues, whatsoever they may or may not happen to be, have thus far availed nothing."

"They have brought us two together, Smirt. It may be that before long," the girl said, with an odd, an almost hungry look, "they will bring us a great deal more closely together. There is a quiet little place over yonder—"

"It is that outcome which I desire, my darling, even though it be far more than has been merited by my wit, my fancy, my profundity, and by yet other mental gifts with which a few excellent critics have been so kind as to accredit me—oh, but beyond doubt, through that habitual excess of charity which distinguishes most book reviewers,—and to which, Arachne, I shall not further allude lest I appear boastful. Some day I must show you my press clippings.

Nevertheless, and with all these talents, I have failed thus far, I repeat, in two quests."

"Your modesty really is," she remarked, with conviction, "rather wonderful. But I do like it, somehow. I find it appetizing. And as I was saying, just over yonder—"

"For I know, Arachne," Smirt continued, "I know very well that I adore you. Yet I do not know anything else about you, inasmuch as I have not yet recovered your legend; and I do not know who I may happen to be, either. That is the great drawback to having an over-vigorous and too inclusive mind. It is a mind, Arachne, which embraces a wide variety of subjects with a quickness I cannot possibly follow. So we are both lost, my dearest, we are lost forever, I am very much afraid, in the encyclopædic dreaming of Smirt."

She appeared puzzled now; and she protested,—

"But you yourself are Smirt—"

"That is perhaps true," he admitted. "It is a point upon which one necessarily reserves judgment. Yet who is Smirt?"

"Why, Smirt," the girl replied triumphantly, "is you."

"I do not deny that, Arachne. At least, as a sound logician, I do not deny it outright. Yet I once dreamed, I must tell you, I dreamed, more or less like the philosopher Chuang Tzu, that I was a blue-bottle fly. I was then conscious only of my thoughts, my interests and my beliefs as a blue-bottle fly, and unconscious of my present individuality as a man. I awoke from that dream, and it seemed to me I was myself again—"

Now the girl's innocent brown eyes had become like lovely saucers.

"And why, dear Smirt, should you not be yourself again, after you had waked up, when it was probably just something you ate? And that reminds me—"

"But do you not see my dilemma, Arachne? I cannot be certain whether I belong to the Mammalia or to the Diptera. Still, I do not know whether I was at that time the Peripatetic Episcopalian dreaming I was a blue-bottle fly, or whether I am at this time a blue-bottle fly dreaming I am the Peripatetic Episcopalian."

Then Arachne said, "But all that is nonsense."

"Is it?" Smirt asked, with unconcealed dubiety. "I am not sure. Only a woman is ever sure. And that is because the more honest of you do not pretend to a sense of humor."

"All your devisings are nonsense," Arachne continued. "You play—like a great dear baby—with your plain out-and-out nonsense, and with your silly chop logic, and, above all, you play with your words, so

that no other person can get in even one word edgewise. And yet I rather like that too, somehow. For
how could anybody possibly be a blue-bottle fly?"

"I was about to say—" Smirt began to answer. But
the girl interrupted him, saying shyly:

"Ah, but let us not talk any longer in this open
road, with people coming and going, and staring at
us so all the time. For just over yonder there is a little parlor, Smirt, a very quiet neat place, where we
could talk quite undisturbed, if only I could trust
you not to attempt any liberties such as we might
both regret afterward, because you really do have such
a way with you, dear Smirt, that a girl feels utterly
helpless—"

"You wrong me, my darling. You misunderstand
the nature of a Southern gentleman," said Smirt,
mildly horrified. "A Southern gentleman does not
ever take advantage of an unprotected female, no matter what be the temptation, so I have always heard.
And meanwhile I was about to say—when you interrupted me, Arachne, and began to rub up against me
like a kitten in this way, which, although highly
agreeable, does rather interfere with our conversation—I was about to say, I repeat, that no man can
live happily with any woman who cultivates a sense
of humor. It is a fact for which five explanations occur to me—"

"Then do you explain them to yourself at leisure, dear Smirt, now that I am going out of the lands beyond common-sense, in which I have no estate and no legend."

And with that, the pouting and slightly disappointed looking appearance of Arachne vanished, as irresponsibly as it had arrived.

"Come now," said Smirt, "but this will never do. The girl is simply charming. What is far better, she is charmingly simple. No, I cannot have my adored Arachne thus flickering about like a Jill o' lantern or a Wilhelmina o' the wisp, nor can I myself eternally be travelling everywhither in a jiffy. No, my duty is plain. It is needful that I return to Amit, a god among godlings; and that in Amit I create for Arachne a new legend."

PART SIX

DIVINE STUMBLING-BLOCKS

*   *

*

"*In very much this way has St. George [Egóri] taken over many Pagan legends; and in one of the semi-sacred* bylíny [*v. Bezsónov, Kaleki Perekhozhie*], *he turns round the oaks and the mountains, like Vertodub and Verto-gor. Nevertheless, these* bylíny *may be ranked as fictions: i. e. as facts of real life (as then understood), applied to non-existent, un-vouched, or legendary individuals.*"

* *

THIRTY-SIX

REFLECTIONS OF THE MASTER

*

Now the Shining Ones sat at the ramparts of their supernal home, busied with all sorts of romance making in the approved manner of Smirt. And Smirt, their acknowledged master, the chief of this planet's gods, meditated alone in his temple. Since he could not find the legend of Arachne, he must make her a new legend and a better legend: that was obvious. Meanwhile, when once he had got together the tools of his thaumaturgy, and had ready his paper and his carbon ink and his customary black pen, he found that a number of more or less irrelevant matters invaded his divine mind, to delay creativeness; and about these matters he thought perforce, just to get them out of the way, so that he could settle down to his work with undivided attention.

He did not, he reflected, think about that mortal woman Jane who had been his wife upon Earth, and who had died a great long while ago. He thought, instead, about the churchyard of St.-Peter's-in-the-East, in Oxford, and of its serene beauty under a June sunset; about what had happened, so delight-fully, to Janet Ormerod and Smirt, in the south door-way of this church, a rich specimen of Norman work, badly obscured by the porch with a parvise, or upper story, characteristic of the fifteenth century; about the curious etymology of the word "hearse"; and about the various tariff duties on baking soda, card cases, toothbrushes, cheese, zinc, and Spanish cedar, whether in logs or in sawn planks.

He thought about a dusty disused room and the ancient odors, suggesting an embalmed body, of that room's blue-and-gray-striped, bare mattress, in the while that he and Mrs. Murgatroyd were misbehav-ing themselves; about how odd it was that in his pres-ent dream his power to smell anything appeared to have been remitted; and about the disruption of the Whig party in 1852, when General Winfield Scott carried only four states.

With these matters disposed of, Smirt laid out upon the table ten sheets of writing paper; he scratched his nose; he uncorked his ink bottle; and he sat thinking for a few moments.

Smirt did not think about Jane. To the contrary (as he noted, with continued approval of such ab-stinence) he thought about Beerbohm Tree's fine production of *King Henry the Eighth*, at His Majesty's Theatre in 1911, and about the young girl who played Anne Bullen kneeling to be crowned, in the last scene, with her long neck bent far forward, just as it would bend later over the executioner's block; and about how it was another Jane, a Jane Seymour, who had caused this. He thought about the gargoyles upon Notre Dame; about the silver ring he had bought at the first World's Fair; about the *Washington Post March*; about how at college he saw a road company act *Othello*, and how he coupled later in the night with the woman who had acted the part of Roderigo; about how very pleasant was the combination of Bartlett pears with Gruyère cheese; about how odd it was that, thus far in his dream, he had gone continuously without food; and about an immoral and philosophic Swiss waiter at a small hotel in the small Rue d'Alger, just off the Rue de Rivoli.

Then Smirt thought about Marian, a white blur in her nightgown, as they both waited at their bedroom doors, immediately across the hall from each other, to make sure that the rest of the house was asleep; about the unreliability of rubber as an investment, both in the stock market and elsewhere; about Florence, her perfect body, in which Smirt had been able to find no flaw anywhere except in the slight grossness of her wrist and her ankles, and about her extraordinary tumescence; and about how droll it was that only 261 words should be spoken by Lady Macbeth during the entire tragedy.

After that, Smirt dipped his pen in the ink; he attempted to remove a non-existent small hair, or it might have been a non-existent dust grain, from the point of his pen, with the fore-finger and the thumb of his left hand; and he sat for a while thinking.

Smirt did not think about Jane. He thought about the tax blank (Form III6) upon which you figured out the allowed deduction for royalties already taxed in foreign countries; about how very carefully the Federal Government and the Supreme Court had co-operated to promote disloyalty among authors by tax-ing them with less rationality and with less fairness than were taxed the followers of any other profession; about Perseus in his old age, at Argos, brooding upon that which his eyes alone of living eyes had seen, when the bright shield of young Perseus reflected the face of Medusa; about an anemone noticed in the spring of 1897; about fireflies loitering over a meadow just beyond a railway bridge in the same year of grace; and about goldfish, including comets, shobunkins, moors, telescopes, and fantails.

He thought about prose made fine and elaborate; about Mona Lisa's seniority to the rocks among which she sits, about Ecclesiastes and Isaiah, about the quintessence of dust, about just, mighty and subtle opium, about the drums and tramplings of three conquests, and about the sedulous ape; about American literature, from its acknowledged masterpieces all the way up to mediocre writing; about warm water and mustard, and the better-thought-of book reviewers, and the unfairness of some few of them in compelling you to like them as persons; about that little dark-haired Jeanne, who, for all that she had made away with Smirt's scarf pin in the morning, really did reveal breasts like white apples, and had so justified Theocritus; about a boy whom Smirt had found to be even more wonderful than himself, dead long ago of tuberculosis; about *A Toccata of Galuppi's*, about *Cranford*, about *Proverbs in Porcelain*, about Kenneth Grahame's books, and about *Chastelard*; and about death, which ended all mirth and prettiness utterly, and which made such an excellent literary theme.

Then Smirt looked for and found a small black and yellow blotter, upon which was printed "Promote Prosperity with Printer's Ink," and this blotter he laid upon the topmost sheet of his nice clean writing paper, so that the oil from his hand would not soil this paper while he was writing on it; and he sat for a while thinking.

Smirt did not think about Jane. He thought about how Troilus was rescued by his actual father, Phœbus

Apollo, from the sword of death-dealing Achilles, and was made immortal, and how Troilus could not find upon Olympus, or upon earth, or among the dead, any being so dear to him as was all-hateful Cressida; and how the young demigod returned to her, who was an old woman now, well wasted away in leprosy, and so found contentment. Smirt thought about Athenæus and astigmatism and the Washington Monument and the old-fashioned saloon. He thought, also, about how Lady Jane Crawley (*née* Sheepshanks) after Sir Pitt's death, did not, in so far as Smirt remembered, marry *en secondes noces* either Frederick the Great or Nebuchadnezzar.

Next Smirt thought about katydids, and about the large mole far up on the inside of the left leg of Mrs. Murgatroyd, and about that black-painted tin sign, very rough to the touch, like sandpaper, with gilt letters on it proclaiming that Smirt's father was Attorney at Law; about the green looking dust which buttercups leave upon black shoes; about the knight's move at chess, and about Stonehenge; and about the Man in the Iron Mask (but one had so much wanted Aramis to win out), and about the high percentage of iodine to be found in oysters, and about the two positions of the American flag on Memorial Day.

After that, Smirt dipped his pen in the ink for the second time, and he noted with approval how very cleverly he had controlled his thoughts, keeping them away from any unprofitable and misleading topic.

For Smirt did not ever, he assured himself, think about the mortal woman Jane who had been his wife upon Earth. He thought only about Jane Eyre, and about Jane Austen, and about Lady Jane, the contralto singer in *Patience*; about Jane Shore and about Lady Jane Grey and about Jeanne Du Barry; about Joan of Arc, and reverting to fiction, about Jeanie Deans and about Jehane de St. Pol and about Jenny Wren, the doll's dressmaker; about Jane Addams and about Jeanne d'Albret; about Joan of Navarre, the witch queen, and about wicked Joanna of Naples, and about insane Joanna of Spain, and about Pope Joan, and about Beatrice-Joanna also, in Middleton's *Changeling*.

"It is known, however," said Smirt, conscientiously, "that William Rowley wrote some part of this play."

Then he laid down his black pen without having written one least word of the legend of Arachne, and Smirt buried his face in both his arms, and he began to sob, convulsively, without shedding any tears, because Jane had been taken away from him.

"Master of the Gods," said a girl's voice, "I am called Jane Doe."

"That is a legal fiction; and I prefer Arachne," Smirt answered.

He had lifted his divine head, and Smirt the supreme god sat staring rather forlornly at this school-
girl.

"—And, Master of the Gods, I have come into your
temple to worship you by asking a few questions."

"I remember that there was once a princess," Smirt
replied, as he climbed up on his pedestal, "and you
also, my child, I seem to remember, but in a different
rôle."

*   *

THIRTY-SEVEN

LITURGY OF WORSHIP

*

Therefore," Smirt continued, "do you put your questions as briefly as may be, for I am under bonds to devise the legend of Arachne."

"In one instant, Master of the Gods," replied Jane Doe, as she knelt down before Smirt on his pedestal, —"for I quite comprehend that you are a busy deity now that you are devising the legend of Arachne. But the members of my class in comparative religion have been asked to get in touch with a number of prominent deities of this country, and as a member of my class in comparative religion I have chosen you from a list of the prominent deities of this country. I know that as one of the prominent deities of this country in the profession of creating you are quite busy, but I would appreciate it very much if you would have the kindness, as one of the most prominent deities of this country, to answer me a few questions about your profession of creating."

"Well, so that your questions be brief, my dear—"

"Where, Master of the Gods, did you receive your education before you took up creating as a profession? Which one of your own creations do you like best, and what are your hobbies when you are not working at your profession of creating? How long had you taken up your creating as a profession before you became one of the most prominent deities in this country? Before you became one of the most prominent deities in this country why did you take up creating as a profession? Now that you are one of the most prominent deities in this country, to what do you attribute your success as one of the most prominent deities in this country in creating as a profession? How do you advise young people who want to take up creating as a profession to get started in creating as a profession and to become one of the most prominent deities in this country who are engaged in creating as a profession? And ought I to let my boy friends, I do not quite know how to put it, but with every precaution, of course, or do you think it better for a girl to wait until she is married?"

"Well, I would say it all depends. Yes, my child, it all depends. And now do you pardon me, for I must get back to work upon the legend of Arachne."

And Smirt raised his hand in a gesture somewhere between a blessing and a farewell.

"Yet as one of your most devout worshippers," replied a professor of biology, as he too knelt before Smirt's pedestal, "I think it imperative, now that you have taken up creative work, for you to present to our university an autographed Arachne. We now have over 2500 creations, each and every one of which bears the name of the gifted and gift-giving deity who made it up out of his own head. We beseech you, whensoever you visit China, to honor with a brief epiphany the splendid student body of the University of Wen-Ching. We entreat you, O Master of the Gods, to devote a day or two to the scenic beauties of Peeping."

"Why, whatever do you mean, my worshipper?" said Smirt.

"I mean, Divine Master," the kneeling professor replied reverently, "that the University of Wen-Ching, in Peeping, China, is American supported."

"Even in its grammar," Smirt assented.

"I mean also, Divine Master, that by many authorities Wen-Ching is regarded as a most important factor in the development of our next generation. Although founded as a Christian institution, and though loyally supported by every denominational missionary, the activities and teaching of Wen-Ching are approved by non-Christian leaders likewise. Wen-Ching is co-educational. Through all the national disorders of recent years Wen-Ching, under the untiring supervision of Professor More-cock, has gone along undisturbed. It follows that we all think you ought to honor us with an epiphany at Peeping; and we find it obligatory for you to send us, by to-day's post, an autographed Arachne."

But again Smirt had lifted his divine hand in protest.

"I cannot grant your logic," said Smirt, "and in consequence I cannot grant your requests either. No, I desire for you all good luck at Wen-Ching, and at Peeping also, because I recognize the value of a sound classical education. But I will not give away my creations gratis: the tithes of my temple must be kept up. And besides that, enjoyable as I have found your adoration, I do have to create the legend of Arachne—"

"That is an excellent idea," remarked the young man in a snappy gray suit of Kolledge Kustom Kut Klothes, "for the Imperial Typewriter Company is now embarking on a campaign in which it is proposed to use six well-known deities. So pray permit me to straighten your coat sleeve. Look a little to the left, with the chin the least bit farther up, if you do not mind, and now, just a trifle more pleasant, please, splendid, that will do nicely, you can see the proofs Tuesday morning."

"But—" Smirt replied, ineffectively.

"Our plans," the young man explained, "require a personal portrait in which you are seated at the Imperial Portable Typewriter, O Master of the Gods. We beseech also a letter from you pointing out the extreme utility of our machine and how effectually it can be carried about and used under all circumstances. The company takes pleasure in presenting you with one of the newest models of the Imperial Portable Typewriter—"

"But—" Smirt remarked.

"—Upon which," the young man continued, "you can finish the legend of Arachne in no time at all. Your photographs and your letter will be reproduced and distributed to twenty thousand Imperial dealers, from coast to coast, and we will tie in with your publishers to advertise the legend of Arachne as one of our products."

"But," Smirt repeated, "before that I must create the legend of Arachne."

"Yet do you first allow me, O Master of the Gods," said an elderly butcher, "to tender my sincere and my most hearty congratulations on your superb craftsmanship in the legend of Arachne. How I chortled and chuckled over the cleverness of the dialogue and your deep understanding of the humors and ironies of life! Will you please be good enough to copy out and autograph for me the second paragraph upon page 120, and thus add an inestimable treasure to my collection of your creations?"

"Will you not give me a signed photograph?" asked the baker, "for I think very highly of the legend of Arachne. It grips the reader."

"In this manuscript," said the candlestick maker, "I have set forth my views upon Sovietism, sin, silver, suicide, Siam, and civic sanitation. I believe that this manuscript will peculiarly appeal to the gifted creator of the legend of Arachne. So do you kindly read it, and make the necessary alterations, not later than next Wednesday, and then tell me to what publisher I ought to send it."

Thereupon came bustling into Smirt's temple Tom, and Dick, and Harry, along with Madame Quelquechose and Señora Etcetera and Lady Ampersand, and after these came Anon and Ibid and the world and his wife, and Mrs. Murgatroyd came also.

"Master of the Gods," said Tom, Dick and Harry, speaking in unison, "now that we are eighteen, sex has become very wonderful to us, and we desire to talk about it. We think, Master, that there is something about great minds such as you and we possess which remains eternally naïve: only fools become accustomed to miracles. The Puritan, the dunce, and the rustic start out by sneering; they end by accepting mutely. The radio, the Venus of Milo, the electric light, the overture to Tannhäuser, Arcturus, fornication, and Christopher Marlowe are all very obvious to such lost souls. But the genius says: 'I do not understand how it is possible. Of course I must believe, because I can see and hear, but it remains none the less incredible.' Because he has genius he lives in unending wonder. The fool quickly accepts and as quickly forgets. Take sex, for example—"

It was a mandate at which Smirt sighed a trifle impatiently.

"Ah, but why not," said Smirt, "take something else? Why do you striplings not ever take anything else as your hackneyed theme?"

"Because, Master," replied Tom, Dick and Harry, "the ordinary man flops on the most beautiful of all beautiful things, the female body; he assaults it with his own body; he tumbles off: and he forgets the entire matter, all in five minutes. But a genius can pour out all his libido on the altars of Venus and never fail to be puzzled, to be filled with a glorious wonderment, or to be amazed always anew. The miracle fascinates him; it arouses both unbelief and a passionate adoration. He likes it; he wants to do it again. That, Master, is what we think about sex. That is why we believe that each one of us four is a genius. Are we not right?"

Smirt inclined his divine head gravely. And he said, even more gravely:

"Well, it all depends, my dear lads. In any event, your dicta upon this most vital and highly important subject are of such interest that I must now avert from them with a great deal of sincere regret, in order that I may create the legend of Arachne. And so, some other day perhaps—"

"Whenever I talk with people who have read only the legend of Arachne," Señora Etcetera declared—"whereas I of course have read all your books, over and yet over again—then I get rattle-headed. It seems to me that they have not found in your books what I have found. Which proves, does it not, that I am more sensitively sensitized? Yes, oh, yes indeed! Some people have wicked minds. You are naughty at times, O Master of the Gods, but I worship you whole-heartedly, because you are amusing at all times, which is the very nicest thing that a god can be."

"But I, I adore you, Master of the Gods," remarked Madame Quelquechose, "and I wish that you could be wholly mine. Of course you do not really exist. You are just a beautiful dream I have dreamed."

"Do you think so?" said Smirt, dubiously: for this notion seemed rather to complicate matters.

"Oh, but beyond doubt," replied Madame Quelquechose; "and I am glad of that, too, because in real life I am deeply in love with a quite different kind of person. Monsieur Quelquechose thinks most highly of him. So he fits into my reality; but you fit into the dream."

"Yes, Smirt the supreme god is a dream," said Lady Ampersand, "and I am his living quotation. Every time my lips part in talking, his sweet words fall therefrom. If that wicked girl in the fairy tale had but read the fine books of Smirt, she might so easily have dropped his lovely words instead of those horrid toads."

"And Smirt is my dream also," put in Mrs. Murgatroyd. "I think his books are perfectly wonderful. I am very proud to have known him before he became divine. I tell everybody about him. I simply cannot imagine what it was I saw in Murgatroyd."

"I also," said the world's wife, "I have dreamed about the beautiful high brow, the dark Byronic curls, the refined Grecian nose, the firm chin, and the sensitive mouth which reveals only enough to make its hearers hungry for yet more of Smirt. O lovely Master of the Gods, I am wholly glad that I dreamed you. Now do you tell us about your philosophy of life."

Then they all cried out confusedly:

"What will be the future trend of Southern literature?"

"Do you compose on the typewriter? Do you dictate? And do you write in the morning or in the evening?"

"Is alcohol injurious, and are we, or are we not, upon the verge of a vast spiritual awakening?"

"Tell us frankly which one of your own books do you like best?"

"What about correspondence courses in short story writing, who is your favorite author, and ought children to be taught to believe in Santa Claus? Why is the *American Spectator*? Do you write every day or do you wait for inspiration to move you?"

"What, Smirt, are your religious beliefs in not over two hundred words? What constitutes your ideal of true womanhood? When is your next book to appear and what are you going to call it?"

All these questions they asked confusedly without waiting for any answer. And all the while, too, the public at large became more pallid. The colors went out of their faces and out of their hair and out of their clothing also. They became like ghosts, nor were they any longer distinct in outline. They were like blown tatters of fog, they were like mere cigarette smoke, now that, very much as Airel and Elair had vanished, so did a wind carry away, gently, all except one of the public at large; but as they passed out of Smirt's tem-plc they still shrilled and chirped and twittered their questions.

"Master of the Gods," said the young girl who remained in Smirt's temple, "I am called Dorothy—"

"I prefer Arachne," Smirt answered, sighing.

"—And, Master, you did not ever answer my letter—about your lecturing."

"I remember that there was once a princess," Smirt said, with sigh number two, "and you also, my child, I seem to remember, but in a different rôle."

* *

THIRTY-EIGHT

A LECTURE FOR DOROTHY

*

I remember you perfectly (Smirt continued.) Writing in behalf of the two literary societies of your college, you, my dear Dorothy, have asked if, and when, and at what fee per evening, I would agree to lecture in your college auditorium, as to whatsoever topic I may elect—although you aidfully added you were certain that "a message" from me concerning Modern Trends in Literature would be of deep interest to the students, the faculty, and their friends,—and you have asked also that I advise you whether "anything along this line" would be "worth my while."

To be frank with you (Smirt went on, as he lighted a fresh cigarette, and leaned back, rather more comfortably, on his pedestal) it would not be worth my while—nor your while either. I still marvel, with an aged and resigned wonder, at the quaint notion that some possible profit is to be got, by anybody concerned, from inducing the professional man of letters

to lecture. You would not ask in just this off-hand
fashion, I imagine, that same author to perform upon
the college auditorium piano, before the students,
the faculty, and their friends, or to adorn the auditorium walls with mural paintings. You would incline, first, to make sure of his musical gifts or of his
ability to paint.

Nor—and this is an analogue even more exact—
nor would you address to that author an invitation to
appear, upon a set evening, before the students, the
faculty, and their friends, and thereupon to enliven
the gathering by singing *Céleste Aïda* or *The Last
Rose of Summer.* The singer and the author (along
with the actor, the lecturer, and the crossword-puzzle
maker) do utilize a common material, in that each of
them employs words; and yet, after hardly more than
a half-hour's steady thinking about this matter, you
will begin to divine, my dear Dorothy, that all these
persons use words variously, in accord with the tenets
and the limitations of perceptibly different arts.

I grant that members of a race so multifarious as to
produce both men and women may be able in more
than one art. It is humanly possible, I mean, for an
author to "speak" passably: but the event is rare.
Looking back through a long and terrible vista of
auctorial lectures, I can recall one woman writer who
"spoke" (upon I have no least notion what subject)

with a simple and cordial virtuosity such as kept me through a contented hour's length mentally purring. I delight, because of that well-nigh unique memory, to recognize, in Zona Gale, an actually accomplished writer who actually could "speak," and with whom "speaking" was a fine art finely practised. To the other side, without any unwise name-calling, I think of a woman who had published sundry volumes of the most bland and charming essays ever penned by an American, and of her dictatorial, her sullen, and her gross conduct of the one lecture I was fated to hear her deliver. That was an all-tragic afternoon, which robbed me forever of any further pleasure in the writings of an over large and regrettably vocal snapping turtle.

The epiphany of this harridan remains to me, I repeat, a continued distress—and yet, only in degree. For how many other soul-chilling, how many haggardly vivacious females do I recall, all of whom "spoke" upon the inconsequent ground that they knew more or less about writing! And with what circumspection did I shun their books afterward!

As to male authors, I clap one hand on my heart, and rest the other hand on the family Bible, in the while I protest that every one of them whom I have heard "speak" showed then at his worst. Even did he orate smoothly, without fidgets, without forlornly clearing his throat, and without too often seeking respite in the ice-water pitcher, yet did his inane utterance glister, as it were, with the greasy high-mindedness and the tin-plated goodfellowship which no public speaker can very well avoid. In most cases this did not matter, because the majority of persons who write badly enough to be in demand as lecturers are charlatans or bunglers at all seasons: but to observe bedizened in any such humbug the man of real talent is painful.

It is painful because there drift about, in that more rarefied air of the platform, some fumes, some straying gases, which affect the intelligence. A few victims these effluvia reduce to gulping, to the conscientious coughing of Camille, or to blank merciful unintelligibility: but the more hapless they intoxicate *coram populo*. And as a pragmatic people, we have learned to accept this fact. We do not note, as a rule, how wildly does the babblement made upon platforms by the habitués of this dire eminence differ from the at least relatively sane speech of our school-teachers and our politicians and our clergy in their private life. It is tacitly understood by everybody that, when "speaking," the professional "speaker" expects his sentiments to be received at a liberal discount, and upon this full dress occasion will introduce no one of his beliefs in their working clothes.

All oratory I, in brief, (with the appropriate glibness of a person who knows nothing whatever about it) assume to be an art with its own formal conventions. But I am certain it is an art through which none may attain to self-expression; and in this respect it differs by a world's width from authorship.

I mean that the writer, at his desk, so long as he toils over the progress of composition, can imagine that somewhere outside the door of his study an intelligent and sympathetic audience, well worth all painstaking, awaits his masterpiece. To that "acute but honorable minority" he can address himself freely, with glad confidence, and without compromise.

Let no such happy man turn lecturer! I entreat, with an emotion, you may note, which rises naturally into blank verse. For when once this misled visionary mounts the platform, he becomes conscious that no supermen assemble to honor him. His flesh and blood audience is not even, in any real sense, sympathetic: at best, it stays receptive, waiting to be wooed, waiting to be roused into approval of him, by its own standards. He perceives, too, that this audience (in common with any audience ever assembled anywhere) is not, or at least is not pre-eminently, intelligent. As a whole it very much prefers, it demands, and it visibly awaits, those sleek false formulæ which the

wise honor with lip service in public. So the entrapped word-monger begins with his "Ladies and
gentlemen," and after loosing this trial balloon of
fancy he is soon well under way in imaginative
truckling.

I have been privileged at odd times to sit, serene
and dutiless, upon the rostrum whence some less
lucky author was presently to address his public; and
I have considered his raw material. Not ever did the
spectacle prove exhilarating: never did I covet his
job. To be applauded by such people seemed to me,
in all honesty, compromising. Sloth, and ostentation,
and a timid lechery, and light-headedness, and self-
conceit, and disapproval, and inattention, and boredom, I found over-plainly inscribed on the raised
faces turned usward. And in yet more liberal quantities, of course, was to be seen gaping at us that dull-
mindedness which continues to betray an uncoerced
people into paying for, and even into using, tickets
for a lecture.

Now I daresay, my dear Dorothy, that these are the
prevailing traits in any human assemblage, of the
better sort, when one views it without prejudice. I
admit that, in the last outcome, it is to just this partially cultured audience every American artist must
appeal. But my point is that the American author
who is seduced into lecturing cannot any more evade

this discouraging fact, inasmuch as night after night he encounters a roomful of his own atrocious admirers, in the persons of you and of the other flibbertigibbet students and of the depressed faculty and of their frowsy friends—and, in brief, of the public at large.

He regards perforce this squatted herd of Mammalia at close range; and no further delusion is possible. Here are the butcher, the baker, and the candlestick maker, here are Tom, Dick and Harry, but above all here are Madame Quelquechose and Señora Etcetera and Lady Ampersand and Mrs. Murgatroyd. The dream-vendor—the purveyor of all beautiful and lofty imaginings, the promoter of divine dissatisfactions—stands face to face with the public at large. He sees immediately before him his paymasters, in the sensual, the bored, the chuckleheaded, and the smug middle-classes of an imperfectly civilized nation, upon whose favor and whose shifty whims he and his famousness and all our national art are dependant, at the last pinch.

The point is, furthermore, that no intelligent person in such circumstances will elect to speak with intelligence. Instead, "subdued," as the phrase runs, "to what he works in," he will cannily assume the thin virtues, the high-minded illogic, and the false good-humor which all better-thought-of Americans admire; he will prattle; and he will thus earn his lecture fee honestly, by purveying the sane and edifying entertainment he promised.

But the more wise, the more cautious writer, remains snug in his study, at play with his words, and happily imagining that he addresses an all-worthy audience. That audience is in some sense the masterwork of every writer's invention. That audience does not exist anywhere in flesh, and at bottom he knows this. But in his bemused fancy that audience exists clearly enough throughout the while that he writes, and for that while it contents him.

* *

THIRTY-NINE

THE OLD DIFFICULTY

*

Then, why, Master of the Gods," asked the girl Dorothy, when Smirt had ended his speaking, "are you not contented?"

"But I am contented," said Smirt. "Did I not just tell you that it contents me to imagine I have my suitably appreciative audience?"

"And why," this crop-headed, red-haired girl continued, "do you tell lies?"

Smirt looked at her; and he smiled slowly. Smirt said:

"Because I am not any longer young, my dear. For a middle-aged person of my special sort there is no refuge except lying. He must persuade himself at least, and if possible other people, that he has attained something which does not exist."

"And what is that thing, Master?"

"But I have just told you," Smirt replied, "that this never found thing is an appreciative and worthy audience. Young people do not have to bother about this requirement, because every young person is his own audience. You may tell me that such is not the case with young women; and that you speak truthfully you will no doubt believe for some years to come. A young man, at all events, regards himself with unfailing gusto, with a delight and a reprehension which are vivid; he perceives that the one creature with whom he is familiar is an interesting creature. Ah, but by-and-by, out of the kindness of his heart, out of altruism, a young man here and there desires to reveal this absorbingly interesting creature to his fellow beings; and the rest of that no longer young man's life becomes a continued failure in this attempt. So does each one of us who is in some sort an artist seek his audience; and no one of us ever finds it."

"I do not understand you, Master. Everybody has an audience whenever she needs an audience. People look at me and they listen to me—or at least the young men do—"

"They would, my dear, for you have a clear complexion and fine lips and nothing whatever to say with them. I remark all this in your praise, because thinking is a fungus growth which rapidly infects youth and destroys it."

Dorothy, smiling a little, looked up at Smirt sidewise. She said by-and-by,—

"And is it good to be young, Master?"

"I do not know," Smirt returned, after weighing the matter rather carefully. "For it is uncomfortable to be young, and it is silly to be young, and it is unsatisfactory to be young no longer."

"I do not understand that," said the girl, pondering, "for a thing must be either good or bad."

Smirt looked at her ruefully. "You," he remarked, "you are the sort of audience I find everywhere. It is to people who believe such untrue and immoral axioms that I must try to explain Smirt. It is like trying to explain the principles of wireless telegraphy to a deaf and dumb Abyssinian, to a person who does not know any more about the language I am speaking than I do about wireless telegraphy. In a general way, of course, I have followed its evolution down to the present day, from the theoretical work of Clerk Maxwell in 1865, and the first experimental proofs of Heinrich Hertz in 1887; but I do not pretend to be an expert in wireless telegraphy. No, I am merely Smirt: I have my good and bad moral qualities, very much as I have my teeth and my knack for phrase making, but I am neither virtuous nor wicked, any more than I am dental or verbal."

"But——" said the red-haired girl.

"No, my child, you are quite wrong. No, I am Smirt, I am a special and indivisible medley, a mixture in which, I pause to assure you, my egotisms are neither more nor less an ingredient than are my bicuspids or my epigrams. And I cannot communicate Smirt, I cannot make him comprehensible to the dull-minded gods or to the flighty-minded public at large. That, child, is the old difficulty, the enduring difficulty—that I can find for myself no really appreciative audience in the universe as it is now constituted; and that I must put up with being worshipped by adorers who do not even know what I am talking about."

Whatever had been on the tip of Dorothy's tongue, you now saw, she had reconsidered saying it. The girl asked, instead,—

"Yet is it necessary, Master, always to be talking about yourself?"

"But of course, dear child, that is necessary; that is unavoidable. For I am an artist. And every artist has his own special temperament which colors his work, his perceptions, his thoughts, his doings, and his talking, with an unique tinge. He perceives nothing, he can think about nothing, and of course he speaks nothing, which is not in some degree egoistic. Homer, in brief, is always Homeric."

The girl Dorothy reflected. "And is it good to be an artist?"

"Why, but how should I know, my dear? I have

never been anything else. I would put it that the lark turns to his singing inevitably, because both he and it are larks; and he does not speculate whether he might have lived more contentedly as a horse, or it might be as a hippopotamus, in so far at least as any lark has discussed the matter with me personally."

Now the girl shook her sleek round red head in a forlorn fashion. And she said:

"No, Master of the Gods, I do not understand you. For it seems to me that you talk nonsense, that you are at large pains to talk nonsense—"

"That is urbanity," Smirt pointed out. "It is a sort of armor."

"—And yet, under it all, you are unhappy, Master of the Gods. At no instant are you freed of unhappiness."

"And that, my dear," said Smirt lightly, "is logic. For I have only my disciples, who make parodies, and my worshippers, who address to me the wrong sort of anthems."

She came to him, touching his hand. "Can I not help you, Master?"

Now his mouth widened at each end, a trifle uglily, he suspected, like the mouth of a mastiff. Smirt spoke with deliberate harshness.

"For ten minutes, Dorothy, or it might be for the quarter of an hour, I could make use of you. I could employ you as one does a drug. You are young. You are female. That suffices."

She replied gravely: "Let it suffice. For it is not right that you should be unhappy, Master of the Gods."

He looked at her then in half quizzical admiration. "These are suggestions which pain me," Smirt said. "You are an idiot. Compassion is not really the same thing as justice and piety and philosophy. Yet I am nine-tenths—no, I am ninety-nine-hundredths—in love with you. For that reason I shall not defile your sublime idiocy. No; it is right enough that I should be unhappy. And I shall get along, somehow, so long as I avoid *hubris*."

After that, Smirt kissed the girl Dorothy, with cool and urbane affection. Then he dismissed her from his temple, saying,—

"Get along with you! swoosh! shoo!"

—Which was all very well, Smirt reflected; and which displayed that proper respect for womanhood such as graces any Southern gentleman who is past his prime. The only trouble was that the girl's talking had revealed to Smirt his pre-eminent need to be rid of Smirt's pre-eminence.

PART SEVEN

TOUCHES POETIC JUSTICE

* *

*

"No specific reason can be assigned for the disappearance of the terms 'thou,' 'thee' and 'thine' from current speech. These words were familiar usage in Old English, but during the Middle English period were gradually superseded by the plural 'you' (or 'ye') and 'your.' On 30 August 1924 the Prince of Wales dined with President Coolidge at the White House, returning in the evening to Syosset, N. Y."

*   *

FORTY

REPRESENTING THE FIRM

*

Come now," said Smirt, "but this is intolerable. It is not only that I can find nowhere upon earth, nor in any supernal region to which I have yet had access, my fit audience. It is not only that even in Ámit the public at large pursue me with the slur of fond admiration, and instead of delighting in my wit, my profundity, and my graceful prose style, delight only in my opinions as to topics about which I have no opinions. These troubles I can face with philosophy: they are common to all persons of genius. Another trouble goes deeper. Another trouble is unique. I alone of creative artists have been afflicted with divine disciples, and the Shining Ones have caught my manner far too successfully. All is urbanity and loveliness and topsy-turvy folk-lore and wellbred despair, with Smirtlings travelling toward all points of the compass upon irrational quests. All human life has become a bare-faced plagiarism from my books."

He turned to the vast stores of his scholarship for the requisite goetia. He invoked the All-Highest in the appropriate formula, and hardly had he so much as spoken the words *"Shem hamporasch"* when the archangel Azrael appeared.

"Now but this is indeed a surprise," said Smirt, cordially shaking hands with the Dark Angel, "and a most delightful surprise, to be sure, for all that it was not exactly you whom I summoned."

"All-Highest & Company present their compliments, Smirt. They acknowledge your favor of even date, the contents of which have been duly noted."

"Ah, yes, for I may tell you in confidence, my dear Azrael, this is an affair of some importance, involving as it does the cosmos, the scheme of human life, and the reorganization of all current celestial government. I am ready now to help your principals with a semi-official report, with a well-thought-out bill of complaints, and with a vast deal of constructive criticism."

"A personal interview is not possible, Smirt. All-Highest & Company present their compliments and desire not ever again to be bothered with your nonsense. You will pardon my use of the word 'nonsense,' I am sure, upon the understanding that I act simply as a messenger."

"I quite understand, my dear Azrael. Nevertheless,

I have here"—and Smirt took out his forty reis piece —"omnipotence within limits. My wishes within limits cannot be denied."

"But I," said Azrael, in naïve surprise, "am the Angel of Death. I do not know anything about omnipotence. I have never encountered it. Of what nature is this omnipotence?"

Thereupon the Angel of Death looked Smirt full in the face and considered Smirt gravely.

And Smirt a bit hastily offered him a cigarette, because Smirt did not at all like being looked at by those pensive, dark, and yet pitying eyes, whose appraising of Smirt troubled him as no other thing had ever before troubled Smirt. And it was a bother too that Azrael remained so indeterminate in appearance as to be rather more like a cloud than an archangel.

"In fact," said Smirt, "let us change the subject. You do not smoke? You are wise. It is a quite dreadful habit. So your principals thought I was talking nonsense. Dear me, but these business men! these executives! They are fine fellows, in their way, but one cannot make them understand the bare rudiments of common-sense or of sound art. I merely pointed out to your firm that their conduct of the universe, aside from being irrational in some respects, was in yet other respects unæsthetic."

"That is true," replied Azrael, with the air of one who consults a memorandum. "Yes, that has been reported. You required also, Smirt, that the affairs of the universe should henceforward be conducted without order or system."

"Oh, but come now!" Smirt answered, with the promptness of a sound logician. "Let us distinguish! I did but explain to your firm that they were conducting the universe in a seditious manner, not only from the point of view of my religion as an Episcopalian, but likewise from the point of view of my most carefully thought-out theories concerning art. For it is the function of art to interpret and to comment upon life. Now a foreordered and sensibly conducted universe, as I made clear to them, affords no ground for unfavorable comment and needs no special interpreting. It both explains and justifies itself. It offers the most brilliant genius no least pretext for being tolerant and urbane and ironic."

"You required also, Smirt, that the planets should be remolded and mankind attired differently. You lectured the Creator of all things upon the laws of creation, and the Lord of all evil you instructed in the first principles of evil."

"Well, and why not?" Smirt asked reasonably. "I have done a good bit of book reviewing in my day."

"But above all, Smirt, you talked. You talked and

you talked and you talked. You talked so endlessly, it has been reported, that All-Highest & Company could not even guess at what you were talking about."

Smirt resorted first to his cigarette and, after that, to entire frankness.

"In fact, Azrael, I was not greatly impressed by the intellectual grasp of either of your principals. And I did suggest that the firm ought to fall in with more modern ideas. I advised your principals, for the sake of their own good repute, to make of their universe a meaningless muddle wherein each human life becomes a hopeless and richly colored adventure, very much as it is in all my books. And out of the kindness of my heart I threw in a few other suggestions— rather informally, you know, and just as they occurred to me."

"You appear to have done that," Azrael conceded. "It was like, they report, the never ending and senseless and quite unendurable noise of a blue-bottle fly."

"It was like what!" said Smirt. "Oh, but never mind!"

"Like a blue-bottle fly," Azrael told him, with relish.

"I heard you the first time. I am not deaf, my dear Azrael."

"But you asked me, Smirt—"

"Well, and if I did, there is no earthly sense in repeating things over and over again. It sounds doddering. It is not sensible. Nor is it sensible, I can now see, to argue with such obsolete survivals as a Personal Creator and a Personal Devil. They prefer, it seems, to cling to their out-of-date and quite inartistic notions. To such hidebound conservatism there is no reply. They have my permission to jog on in the old rut. So now that is settled, Azrael. Let us dismiss the unpleasant topic. Let us stop talking about insects, for I have a grievance far above bugs."

Then Azrael spread out, almost wearily, those great shadowy hands which had conquered Cæsar and Tamburlaine also; and Azrael sighed dejectedly.

"What is it, Smirt, that you now desire?"

"I desire, in the first place, to point out that all my books are registered under the copyright law of 1909 —including, of course, the amendment added on 24 August 1912. Nevertheless do the Shining Ones infringe these copyrights daily. They dramatize my stories, they pilfer my best phrases, they have turned my superb notions into flat reality. I am surrounded by apes, pirates and plagiarists; and I desire, Azrael, to consult a competent lawyer."

"Then why, Smirt, do you not do so?"

"But how is that possible? In the romantic fine world which I invented there were no such humdrum

244

creatures as modern lawyers. It follows that in the planet patched up by my imitators there are no lawyers, and I in consequence am bereft of legal advice."

"That, Smirt, is called poetic justice. You have created a world of your own. And you find it to be even less habitable than the world from which you escaped."

"Again, Azrael, I would distinguish. It is merely that I respect my art, and gave over a lifetime to its perfection. To-day my most novel devices have been made clichés, my most killing paradoxes are axioms. My books have become mere reportorial realism now that all human life is modeled after my books; and I decline to put up with any such concatenation of annoyances."

Thus speaking, Smirt sank back into a sitting position at the foot of the copper pedestal from which he had been answering the petitions of his adorers; and he waved both his hands in a gesture equally emphatic and graceful. Smirt remarked gaily:

"In brief, my dear fellow, I yield to that stupidity against which the very gods are powerless because it has infected them through and through. I accept, without further comment, the queer tastes of All-Highest & Company. So now, Azrael, now let my dream end, and let me return to my own name, whatever that may be, and to my accustomed habitation upon Earth."

"All-Highest & Company present their compliments, Smirt; and consider that you and your like have done enough mischief upon Earth."

That was an announcement which raised Smirt's eyebrows as far as urbanity and his facial muscles permitted.

"It is true," said Smirt, "that to exemplify the urbane, day in and day out, among a nation which is not capable of being urbane at any time, does stir up some little, quite natural envy and irritation. Some day I must show you my press clippings. Yet the backwardness of America, I submit, is no sound reason for my being left in the middle of a distasteful dream, a dream in which I have no audience except the supreme powers of heaven and the public at large, and am forced every day to consider a worldful of my own notions as they have been misunderstood and travestied by the Shining Ones. You compel me to point out that in plain fairness you, who are the Angel of Death, should at the very least rid me of my divine plagiarists."

The Dark Angel spoke gravely. His unstable and not ever quite clearly seen face, you imagined, was compassionate, in the while that Azrael said:

"To all living creatures, Smirt, I bring death. To

246

the Shining Ones, when they have fallen away from their stewardship and have become tax-payers to the most rigorous of assessors, I shall bring death in due course. But not as yet."

And at that, Smirt shook his head, without feeling called on to hide his disapproval. "These excuses, Azrael, this mere playing for time," Smirt admitted, "I do not find satisfactory. I must tell you that, in all frankness. Beyond that, of course, an urbane person —howsoever disappointed and howsoever grieved, Azrael, by your strange conduct—must elect not to embarrass you by discussing your shortcomings to your face. I dismiss the unpleasant topic. I require merely that you rid me of the public at large, who leave me no peace, not even in the eternal city of Amit."

"Of all human follies," said Azrael, gently and meditatively, "I shall make an end by-and-by. But not as yet. Not even of you, Smirt, and of your continual babbling, may I make an end at this time—no, not as yet. The worlds take shape, the worlds swarm with life, and the worlds perish, as All-Highest & Company work out their design. And yet, from out of the wreckage of each world as it perishes, arises an odd sound, which is at once a taunt and a giggle and a questioning and a sneer; and I may not silence that little, that rather nasty noise—not quite as yet."

"That sound, my dear Azrael," Smirt explained, "is

247

constructive criticism. It is the defiant answer which a small civilized minority flings back at the inescapable and poorly contrived doom of mankind."

Azrael said, with some shortness: "That sound is Smirt. So long as that tiny sound endures, so long will you also endure in your flippant and feverish dreaming. But for no instant longer."

Thus speaking, Azrael, who was already so indeterminate in appearance, now vanished completely. And Smirt merely shrugged over this renewed example of angelic pig-headedness.

"Yet my situation is annoying. I am robbed, I am travestied, and all proper recompense is denied me, in this dream wherein people drop the most uncivil sort of hints about blue-bottle flies. I must get help from Wise Aldemis."

*   *

FORTY-ONE

ALDEMIS PERCEIVES ALL

*

I must get help from Wise Aldemis," Smirt repeated.
And he wondered who this Wise Aldemis might be,
and at what place or time he had heard of her, even
in the same instant that, as a sound logician, Smirt
decided these various problems could not greatly matter, after all, now that he stood face to face with Wise
Aldemis. It was a little confusing, he reflected; but
then dreams were very apt to be like that. It was odd
too that the withered pallid creature stood within a
pentagram drawn with four parallel lines of red and
blue and yellow and green; and at her feet was the
bleached skull of a ram.

"What is it, Smirt," asked the gray woman, at once,
"that you are seeking of Aldemis, with omnipotence
in your pocket?"

"Oh, but come now, dear lady," Smirt replied, "for
me to answer that question would be in some sort to
cast a slur upon that omniscience which you have in

your head. No, no! there is no possible need for me to be telling Wise Aldemis, who already knows everything, that I am now looking for the legend of Arachne; and in consequence I shall not answer your question, and then have you laughing at me for my simplicity."

"In fact, Smirt," said Aldemis, shrewdly, nid-nid-nodding her shrivelled head, "I perceive you are looking for the legend of Arachne."

Then Smirt cried out, in unconcealed admiration, "Did I not say that all things are known to Wise Aldemis!"

"That is true, Smirt; and yet, I admit, on the other hand—"

"So I need not tell you, dear lady, that I am looking for this legend because I promised to restore to the young person in question her lost estate in the lands beyond common-sense."

"Nevertheless—" said Wise Aldemis.

"I need not tell you," Smirt continued, "that since I am omnipotent—within limits—it would be easy enough for me to create anew the milieu of her legend and to put her back in it, in her proper social position, so to speak, if only I knew what her legend was."

"Yes, but—" the gray woman began again to reply.

"No," Smirt concluded, "there is no least need for

me to tell you any one of these things; and it is for that reason I have preferred to implore your aid and your mercy without speaking of these irrelevant matters."

The pale eyes of Aldemis became yet more friendly. She said:

"You have done well, Smirt, for I could never put up with loquacious and ever chattering people—"

"In fact, dear lady, garrulity is the besetting sin of a great many unurbane persons, who must continually be talking and interrupting, and repeating the obvious, and it is precisely this unwisdom I have been careful to avoid in approaching your omniscience."

Then Aldemis said: "You have done, I repeat, well. You would do yet better to stop talking about your taciturnity. And you would do still better, I believe, did you put this Arachne out of your head."

"I almost wish that I could, dear lady," Smirt answered, with a self-tolerant smile, because it seemed amusing to find frailties even in Smirt. "And yet, too, I almost think that, what with one thing and another, if you quite follow me, and inasmuch as I did make an explicit promise to the girl, who seems rather a nice little creature, ma'am, and what with my being a Southern gentleman, even in my sleep, yes, I do almost think that upon the whole I would prefer not to put Arachne out of my head, if it is really just the same to you, dear lady."

"I see," said Aldemis, drily. "I have seen many things. But never did I see a master of gods who looked more like an embarrassed booby."

And Smirt laughed. "I shall not dispute that, Aldemis. You see, she is nothing much to look at, and she has no intelligence at all. Still, I do rather like the way that her head is set on her neck; and I daresay that is it."

—To which Aldemis replied only, "You men!"

Yet, as became a kind-hearted wise woman, she made a magic. She did not know, she explained, about legends, because legends deal with the past and that which has been. "I know only all that is," she admitted, with a proud candor which Smirt admired.

So Aldemis made a white magic, taking up the Six Branches—of ash, of basil, of periwinkle, of sage, of mint, and of vervain—in her right hand; and in her left hand she took salt mingled with ashes. She breathed the Word of the Sylphs. And after she had sufflated the four cardinal points, then into her breathing came that power which first moved above dark waters and breathed into the nostrils of man the breath of life. She made Michael her leader and Sabtabiel her servant. Through the calm of her will she took governance for that while over the spirits of air, through the cunning of her wisdom she restrained for that while the power of the sun, so great was the might of Wise Aldemis. For this was a white magic which had in it the candor, as well as the vigor and the magnanimity, of the world's youth.

*   *

FORTY-TWO

THE WARNING OF ART

*

Now in answer to the white magic of Aldemis came very wonderfully, out of the books of Smirt, the women whom Smirt had created. There was a great company of them: he marvelled that one brain could bear so many beautiful and witty and tender daughters. And now that each glittering phantom reminded him of her legend, as Smirt had contrived it, he wondered also that one brain could invent so many splendid adventures.

They spoke with him, saying severally:

"My legend is more lovely than is the legend of Arachne."

"There is no legend anywhere more beautiful than the fine brain of Smirt has builded for me to live in eternally."

"It is very well that the paltry and threadbare legend of Arachne is forgotten now that my superb legend exists."

"Assuredly the maker of the legend of Arachne, did he yet drag out his uninventive existence, would be put to great shame to-day. Did any power revive him, he would die for a second time, of sheer envy. For he would have perceived Smirt's handiwork. He would have despaired ferociously before the countless perfections of my witty and refined legend."

—To all which, Smirt answered: "Most dear and most adorable of women, it is possible you are right. It seems highly probable that my genius transcends the more modest talents of the creator of Arachne's legend. I admit that, in fairness to everybody, because I am a sound logician. Yet how can I be quite certain about this until I have found the legend of Arachne? Then, and then only, you perceive, can I make my fair comparisons, and laugh without any least rancor at the poor fellow."

Again spoke the glittering and unhumanly beautiful women whom Smirt had created. "Be very glad," they said, "that we were made for the delight of mankind forever. Take pride in knowing that you and no other person made each one of us. Be utterly sure that there are no legends more lovely than are our legends. Do not think about any other legends. Give a loose rein to pride and to self-conceit, dear Smirt, for these only may preserve you, as they preserve all other artists. Consider only your own greatness, and matters may yet go well."

"I like your legends extremely," Smirt replied. "I rejoice in the long years I gave over to your creating. I delight in you, one and all, my immortal offspring. Yet I delight without any vainglory, because modesty has always been with me a distinguishing trait. I cannot conquer it, somehow. Besides that, until I have found the legend of Arachne I lack any standards of comparison. Moreover, the urbane person does not give way to pride and self-conceit. No, let us avoid *hubris*: otherwise, there is no telling. In the third place, I promised to put the girl back in her legend, and a Southern gentleman must keep his word, no matter how soundly he may be asleep. And to conclude with, I do like the way her head is set on her neck."

Wise Aldemis shrugged her lean shoulders, in the instant that all the lovely daughters of Smirt's wit and fancy went back to their improper places in the books of Smirt. Then Aldemis set about a gray magic.

She made upon the ground a circle with strips of kid's skin, she made within this circle a triangle drawn with the stone called ematille. In a brazier she burned willow wood and camphor and brandy, in the while that she pronounced correctly the gray charm of Zariatnatmit, which controls Rimmon and Asmo-

deus. By the four Supreme Names, and by the antago-
nism between fire and water, she compelled the
separating of all substances, even as they were sep-
arated during the forenoon of the day of the world's
making. She took upon her that dreadful power
which divides, and which divides infinitely, beyond
the reach of any man's thought, and in this way did
she divide Smirt from Smirt's erudition.

*   *

FORTY-THREE

THE VERDICT OF ERUDITION

*

When the vapors of this second magic had cleared away, Smirt saw that out of his brain had come seven members of that large host of learned persons who provided Smirt's erudition. They were less lovely than the women whom Smirt had created. And these profound, lean, and fusty scholars declared severally:

"It may be that Arachne is the dawn."

"Philology shows that Arachne is a thunder cloud."

"Beyond doubt, Arachne is the spring, who conquers the darkness of winter."

"Yet it may be as Müller suggests, that Arachne is the evening aurora."

"To my mind, Arachne is quite obviously a grain of sprouting corn."

"By Grimm's law, Arachne must be the moon."

"Arachne is, beyond question, a much later and spurious interpolation."

"Sirs, sirs," said Smirt, "she is no one of these

things, I assure you. This Arachne is merely a young woman who has been dispossessed of her estate in the lands beyond common-sense; and for that reason I desire to know her legend."

"But in order to have a legend, Smirt, it is needful that she should be some one of these things," the learned men then replied in unison. "For all legends concern these matters and no other matters."

"That is possible, sirs, but she does not look like any one of them. No thunder cloud, for example, could well have its head set upon its neck in quite that fashion—"

"You are now talking," said the learned men, severely, "in an unscientific manner."

"Yet the spring, gentlemen, has not any such soft-looking red lips, just parted a little, you know, when she looks up at you and waits for you to speak—"

The learned men said, "Bosh!"

"Nor, my dear sirs, have I ever noticed a grain of corn with precisely such innocent dark eyes, which half doubt you and half laugh at you—"

To that the learned men replied, "Stuff and nonsense!"

Then these learned men took snuff, each one of them from his own horn snuffbox.

"And I wonder, gentlemen," said Smirt, "if upon consultation of the proper books—"

They answered, after putting up their seven snuffboxes:

"We have searched zealously in many books. We have read from cover to cover the Works of Ebenezer Sibly, along with C. J. Paton's *Freemasonry and Its Jurisprudence*, and Gilbert White's *Natural History of Selborne*—"

"You begin well, gentlemen, in a broad field—"

"Also," they continued, "the *World Almanac* for 1925, and Balzac's *Père Goriot*, and Baedeker's *Guide to Switzerland*—"

"Come now, but that is excellent, for there is nothing like thoroughgoing research work—"

"In addition," they concluded, "to the *Bacchæ* of Euripides, two numbers of the *Atlantic Monthly*, George Eliot's *Scenes from Clerical Life*, and Hornblower & Weeks' *Financial Glossary*. But in no one of these books have we found the legend of Arachne."

"Then what next, gentlemen," said Smirt, affably, "can the unparalleled powers of your erudition suggest?"

They replied: "It has been suggested by Charles Kingsley, in his *Glaucus*, that a desultory small treatise cannot well end more usefully than in recommending a few volumes on Natural History, fit for the use of young people. We do not demand that this list shall contain all the best books, but simply the best of which the compiler knows; for Christmas seals were first introduced into this country from Denmark in 1907, and, since 1917, have been distributed every year by the National Tuberculosis Association."

This was a verdict over which Smirt meditated for a good while, before remarking:

"Your statements, gentlemen, appear quite truthful, in so far as they go. They would be most helpful, no doubt, if only I happened to be a desultory small treatise. But as a mere master of gods, I must ask just what do you mean?"

They took snuff again. Then they replied patiently:

"We mean that the Goodwood Races begin on the last Tuesday in July, and last four days. They are held in England, in a private park belonging to the Duke of Richmond, and are very select affairs. In removing stains caused by fruit or fruit juices use boiling water, and then bleach if necessary. The Athenians, however, began the year in June, the Macedonians in September."

After that, these learned men vanished, like candles which have been blown out, as they went back into Smirt's brain. Thus was his erudition restored to him; and thus was he relieved from listening to it himself. And Wise Aldemis now set about a black magic, about the unholy magic of the Cat and the Abtu Fish.

Yet nothing came of this magic, in so far as Smirt could perceive. As he looked about him inquiringly, all seemed as it had been. Smirt wondered then, in half shocked surprise, if the gray woman had failed in her thaumaturgy. He looked at her next; and he found that this third magic was a specially perturbing magic, inasmuch as it had changed Aldemis into the one person whom easy-going and urbane Smirt disliked.

* *

FORTY-FOUR

"LESBIA, ILLA LESBIA"

*

So now Smirt faced Mrs. Murgatroyd, whom alone of all the public at large he found to be wholly detestable, and the fat painted creature said to him at once,—

"I think your books are perfectly wonderful."

"It is you who are wonderful, Mrs. Murgatroyd," he replied, a little shaken; for Wise Aldemis had evoked, at last, the one magic which could always upset Smirt, with its never failing bitterness, and which caused him to forget every other living woman.

Now Mrs. Murgatroyd replied, tittering: "Get along with you, Smirt! For I reckon you say that to most every girl you start a-flirting with."

And Smirt cried out, "For urbanity's sake, woman, do you stop your giggling and your leering at me!"

"La, but did anybody ever hear the like of you, Smirt! and that is a nice way indeed for you to be talking to a lady."

"I cannot help it, Mrs. Murgatroyd. I cannot endure the sight of you, Mrs. Murgatroyd, as a fat walloping old wench. I find unbearable the pink and fussified clothes that are now twenty years too young for you, Mrs. Murgatroyd. And I do not like your lipstick, Mrs. Murgatroyd—no, nor your plucked eyebrows either."

"My, but just listen at the man!" she remarked, equably.

Indeed Smirt rather wondered at himself. There was far too much of this woman, he reflected: yet even nowadays she stayed not unhandsome, in her own excessive way; and in all the many pounds of her, as Smirt knew, there was not one half-ounce of malevolence toward anybody. There never had been.

Nevertheless, Smirt found that his talking went on in a most embarrassing vein of candor. For Smirt was now saying:

"And when you walk, Mrs. Murgatroyd—only, you do not walk, you mince and you totter, like a drunk woman, in shoes that are far too tight for you—then you shake and you wobble and you wriggle in all remote sections. You are like a perambulating pink jelly. There is no cow but would be ashamed of such udders. And as for the waggle of your big broad backside, I never did see anything like it."

"Of course I am a-getting on in life, Smirt," she

agreed placidly. "And you used to could bear the sight of me pretty well, both in and out of my clothes, when the two of us was young."

"That is why I said you were wonderful, Mrs. Murgatroyd. But for you—as you put it—'both in and out of your clothes,' there would perhaps have been no books, no Smirt. For it was through you, my dear Jessica, 'when the two of us was young,' that I learned the meaning of two very common words—of love and of happiness. And afterward I learned the meaning of such words as perfidy and anguish, and of hatred also, Mrs. Murgatroyd. It was a long while before I found out how few people do really know what these words mean."

The gross woman looked at him with placid blue eyes which stayed friendly.

"Such goings-on," she commented, "over that boy and girl nonsense! But we did have a real good time, Smirt; and I liked you a lot better than I ever let on to Murgatroyd."

"But you, Mrs. Murgatroyd, you never knew the meaning of any one of these words. You do not know anything. You have no mind, no heart, no real desires, no syntax—and no decency either, Mrs. Murgatroyd, for in that event you would keep out of my dreams. But you never have kept out of my dreams, no, not in all these years."

Then Smirt began to laugh; and he said:

"In brief, 'when the two of us was young,' I loved you entirely; and you liked me, more or less, for a while; and after that while, you very sensibly married Mr. Murgatroyd. You treated me abominably, Mrs. Murgatroyd; and for every bit of your infamous behavior my gratitude is unbounded."

"You certainly are a case," she remarked, "if ever there was one."

"And I still find you rather incredible, Mrs. Murgatroyd. For you are not merely disgusting to look at. You are far more: you are a compendium of everything I abhor. There is absolutely no standing you. When you babble to me about my perfectly wonderful books, and about how proud you are to have known me before I became famous, and about how you tell simply everybody about me, you incite me to murder. To begin with, I doubt if you ever toiled through one of my books; and if you did, I am quite sure you could make neither head nor tail of my wit and fancy and erudition. There is not under your henna hair-dye the required intelligence."

"You really are," Mrs. Murgatroyd re-affirmed, beamingly, "a case, with that swelled head of yours. Not but what I like a good book when I got the time for it."

And from her left ear she brushed back her so

frankly dyed hair, with the exact gesture of that girl whom Smirt was not able to forget.

"You display upon all occasions," Smirt continued, "the imagination, the ready tact, and the vivacity also, of a York river oyster. Ah, but what a delight it is to say to you in a dream the things that no Southern gentleman can say during his waking hours! And you were always like that, I know—but how well I know it, after meditating upon the astounding fact for years!—you were always like that inside, even when in your youth you had a superficial prettiness. I daresay you were not even especially pretty. And yet, yet, I found in you all beauty, all perfection, all happiness. I found in you a magic and a poison."

Smirt broke off talking. He had strayed, he felt, some little distance from the neat ways of urbanity. So Smirt shrugged. Afterward Smirt said:

"All that I found in you went into my books. And every man who read them has recognized in my young folly, and in my urbane derision of it, a part of himself. My books are you, you, all you! and you have not the wit to perceive it. That which you created, you cannot understand. Oh, and you created me also, teaching me to regard the ludicrousness of myself even more fondly than I did that of other persons—and yet teaching me always to remember you with a grim tenderness. For you were very useful: I

concede that. It is necessary that all poets should love
Mrs. Murgatroyd—*Lesbia nostra, illa Lesbia,* the divine romance which turns of a sudden into a gorilla
grin of irony."

"La, but how you do talk," remarked Mrs. Murgatroyd. "Quite as fine as the letters you used to write
me—and as I often think, if they are not as good as
a circus, Smirt!"

She did not laugh exactly. But her amusement became almost apoplectic.

"You have kept my letters!" said Smirt, shudder-
ing. "That only was needed. Some day your heirs and
assigns will be publishing them, of course, with no
doubt a portrait of you, pretty much as you now are,
for the frontispiece. Yes, that only was needed—my
insane rhapsodies in conjunction with your portrait.
However, I can think offhand of very few women
who are not planning to publish my letters. One volume more or less will not matter. And I desire only
to make the fact plain to posterity that I did not ever
correspond until I had copulated."

After that, Smirt gallantly lifted to Smirt's lips
Mrs. Murgatroyd's plump and small and really, as
he observed with surprise, quite pretty hand.

"It has been an immense comfort to say to you in
this dream, dear Jessica, the things which I could not
say when awake. And for the rest, I am deeply grate-

ful, alike for your kindness and for your charity—in not marrying me, I mean,—and for your turning out to be such a wholly unattractive person afterward. Your memory has been to me an unfailing inkwell. All my heart praises that loveliness which was yours in the eyes of a boy very long ago. I praise likewise your perfidy. I praise above all the inane grossness which you now flaunt in middle life. For these three things have combined handsomely, O far too big and too wobbly and too crudely renovated source of my genius, these things have combined to make me Smirt, Smirt whom the public at large pursue, Smirt whom the gods also revere and imitate."

Thus he boasted; and in the while he was speaking a clock struck thirteen.

"Alas and alack!" said Smirt, forebodingly, "but this is no doubt the appointed hour. And I, of all persons, have incited it. For I have forgotten to be urbane, I have been betrayed into *hubris*."

PART EIGHT

FOR EACH HIS HOUR

* *

*

"Whensoever the Khirghiz pass by Musta-ghata, loftiest of the Pamirs, they fall upon their knees in prayer, for upon the summit of this mountain stands the unapproachable bright city of Janaidar, built in a golden age, and still visible from afar. In Venezuela also Humboldt observed a mountain to be strangely luminous at night, and attributed this phenomenon to the burning of hydrogen gases."

* *

FORTY-FIVE

AT THIRTEEN O'CLOCK

*

In the eternal city of Amit a small onyx clock (which was left over from Tana's cave, Smirt now remembered) had just finished striking thirteen: and before Smirt stood a hooded company of seven huge persons, all robed in ash-colored gray and made ready for travel. Their leader put by his hood; and Smirt saw that this was Arathron.

Brown Arathron said: "So very soon has come the appointed hour. The liquor of the gods is almost gone, there is scarcely a drink left, only a few drops remain to us of the dark beer of Sekmet. My splendors fall away from me as the bright leaves drop pensively from a maple-tree in autumn. There is in my thoughts a smell of winter. I have lived my last hour as a Steward of Heaven. In a little while, I must be leaving forever the city of Amit, wherein all things were perfect, where each day and hour held some form of delight, and everything seemed builded for my pleasure. I had not known until to-day how beautiful is Àmit. It is strange yet to be beholding Àmit, wherein I have gone about always light-hearted, a god among gods."

Then Phul, that huge hermaphrodite who was colored like silver, said:

"The horror of it troubles me, to look upon mortal tax-payers, and to know that is what each fallen god must become. The strivings and the small doings of this planet's people are taxed very heavily by time and by common-sense. I tread, as boldly as may be, down a cold gray path, to live as a tax-payer. I shall not look back. It may be that by-and-by, when I have become an applauded person, perhaps a great statesman or a famous minister of the gospel, some ghost of Àmit may rise to plague me and to draw from me a sigh. I shall shrug then. My thoughts will return to the higher brackets of common-sense, and to time's sur-taxes, and to my allowed deductions in the way of lying and of humbug. I shall again forget Àmit, wherein I went about always light-hearted, a god among gods."

And ruddy Phaleg said: "Time and common-sense have entrapped me. They take a huge toll of my dreams and of my hopes, and of my courage also, now that I must live as a tax-payer. I have wandered about Àmit without any plan. The ghosts of many divine beings went with me. I remembered them all, the gods that were here before me, the gods that are now departing, not ever to return. Our lives narrow down to being well-thought-of. Our glory will never revive. Our strength dwindles, like a little fire under the sun of September, now that befalls the appointed hour. No one of us shall ever live again as a god lives, without paying any taxes to time or to common-sense. We return no more to Amit, wherein each one of us has gone about always light-hearted, a god among gods."

"Oh, but come now," said Smirt, "this is most distressing! Each of us must abide his appointed hour: I concede that. I do not mean to upset any of these cosmic arrangements. Still, I did not intend to incite the appointed hour by forgetting, for just a moment, my urbanity. And I really do think that in this instance All-Highest & Company might have deferred— a little more tactfully, let us say—the stroke of doom. For you and I, my friends, have but very lately put the planet on a properly romantic basis: it was an experiment noble in purpose, an experiment which, I make bold to say, might well have been permitted to work out to its own logical conclusions. Oh, I do not criticize this sudden, this somewhat high-handed, and indeed this virtually idiotic interference with my personal plans. But I do ask, Was it tactful?"

To that, Hagith replied only: "Homage to thee,

Smirt, sole lord of Amit now, dear Master of the Shining Ones! all homage to Smirt, whose names are manifold, whose transformations are sublime, whose purpose is hidden! But a thing done has an end. The appointed hour has struck. So must we depart, because the term of our stewardship is over. So must we cry farewell to you, dear Master, whom we may not imitate joyously any longer."

"I regret that, Hagith, I regret it in all sincerity: for while your efforts to realize my books, to make actual my philosophy and my vision of human living, were not wholly successful, yet I always felt you did your best. Nobody can do more. And besides that, the imaginings of Smirt were perhaps a little beyond your merely divine powers."

Then Arathron said: "That is a true saying, O Lord of Amit. Yet is it equally true that we future tax-payers must go upon the journey appointed for every Shining One."

"Ah, but, but, after all, my dear Arathron," Smirt consoled him, "you are only false gods, you should remember, out of an anonymous German work first published as lately as 1686."

"And are you sure of that, dear Master?" said Arathron, brightening a little.

"I am quite sure," Smirt replied. "You will no doubt find a copy in the Library of Congress."

"To think of that now!" said pallid Ophiel, smiling outright. "We did not know that Congressmen liked to read about us."

"Congressmen, my dear Ophiel," Smirt remarked, "are very often surprising people in all sorts of ways. But, as I was saying, your tenancy of this place has been so much clear gain. As false gods, you were not entitled to be here at all."

"And besides that," said tall golden-colored Bethor, chuckling, "inasmuch as we are only false gods, it does not matter the least bit what happens to us. I see the point, dear Master; and it is a great comfort."

"It should be," said Smirt. "It should delight every one of you to reflect that in defiance of all justice, and in violation of all probability, you have thus had your fling in my dream: for nobody, be he god or man, can hope to have more than that anywhere. As for the impermanency of your divine fling, alas, gentlemen, I can but remark that this is a characteristic of every known form of fling. All greatness is perishable goods: you have perhaps heard that Queen Anne is dead. We must face these losses. You would do well, my dear friends, to observe with what equanimity I am facing your losses at this very moment. For, as becomes a sound logician, I grant that all power and mirth, and all beauty, must perish inevitably, and that I, even I, it may be, shall not endure forever."

But at that, the disemployed Stewards of Heaven cried out, in anguish,—

"Dear Master, pray do not talk to us about any such horrid notion!"

"Well, well," Smirt soothed them, "it may be that contingency is not likely. Still, I am forced, through a proper sense of modesty, to consider that off chance now and again, because the urbane are not ever vainglorious."

Then all the Shining Ones departed out of Amit, a great deal cheered by Smirt's consolations, although Smirt noticed that a black dog, which had a white tail and four white feet, followed after the seven large ash-colored figures and sniffed at fourteen no longer divine legs rather hungrily.

Now at Smirt's elbow stood an untidy young man. And he demanded of Smirt,—

"Did you ever shout into a hurricane?"

"Well, what between one thing and another," Smirt answered, "I am afraid I never quite got around to shouting into a hurricane."

* *

HEIR PRESUMPTIVE

*

My question (the untidy young man continued, frowning) was rhetorical. So please do not put me out by attempting to answer it. I repeat, then, Did you ever shout into a hurricane? That is what I am condemned to do, crying out my just demands for applause and opulence and the homage of all publishers, in the bared teeth of a tempest,—a tempest of mediocrity which engulfs me, and which scatters among its howling winds the cry of my genius, just as mediocrity has always tried to subdue into nothingness the rebellion of superior persons.

It may be that you find the statement extreme, that you think me presumptuous. Yet should gold be esteemed the less golden because it happens to be covered with the slime and muck of unrecognition? I am like Prometheus, now that the vultures of despair eat continually at my liver, for the editors of all known magazines have rejected my manuscripts. With such

bitterness does fate as yet treat me. I intend, nevertheless, to raise a proud head above the stale levels of
mediocrity.

I hear you mutter, impatiently, What the hell is
this jabbering about? It means, Smirt, that all passes.
At an appointed hour the Stewards of Heaven have
passed from their thrones in Amit, and you reign here
alone. At an appointed hour you too will pass; and
I intend thereafter to become your successor here.
I like the looks of the place just as it stands, but when
my time comes I shall liven it up a little, with a copy
of *Das Kapital* and a few strong-backed young
women.

In the mean while I write—oh, God, yes! quite un-
successfully. Somebody or other, as you may remember, calls it spoiling good white paper with strange
black marks. Yet in spite of myself I continue to make
such marks upon paper. I hate writing. It is detestable. It is horrible. It is torture. It is agony. I hate
it like death. Yet as one clings to life, so do I write in
order that I may supplant you, Smirt.

But that is not all of it. I write in order that I may
live. I do not mean, in order that I may support myself: Poppa is quite well-off, on account of our infamous capitalist system. No: I write in order to give
me my one unanswerable reason for existing. And
I seek alleviation of this most dreadful of dreadful

diseases, worditis, in the balm of that applause which is due to my genius. Upon the more foggy side of oblivion my present lack of a suitably appreciative audience becomes just plain agonizing hell.

Yet, *sacre dios,* do you think I complain? No: I say my say and have done. I am a man of few words. That is strange, because I have many sensitive nerves. I feel life in many different forms. I suffer in many variegated forms. So it would appear but natural that I should need many words in order to express myself fully. Yet I do not. I am gifted with concinnity, that most enviable of endowments, which I found only last week in the dictionary.

Do not confound this rare talent with diffidence. An unrecognized writer, like a whore, knows no shame. That modesty which they continually outrage flees from both of them; and this fact is remarked on by their near relatives. When you happen to be very proud, as I am (for we have a family crest), these comments become painful. But I am like a betrayed —no, I mean, a knocked-up and unwed woman; nature has made me pregnant with The Word, and I must have lexicological parturition or die. In childbirth there can be no modesty. Modesty is an attribute of success and attainment: I shall have time to be modest after I have kicked you out of this place and my genius is recognized everywhere. Meanwhile

I demand recognition in vain, and the gnawed crusts of egotism are all that sustain me.

It is very peculiar that I should find life a futile affair, for I am eighteen, with a fine sense of humor, and all women love me. Genius attracts women irresistibly, the canoodling pretty bitches. Then when they get knocked-up they carry on like hell. You would think it was my fault, to hear them talk, and Poppa is as bad as they are. These bourgeois people do not consider that I may be the genius who will interpret the youth of this age, the youth that is so hopelessly muddled, the youth that finds sex to be the actual motivator of all life.

Yet I do not know if this is true, or even just what it means. I often say things like that. They quite upset Mumma. Nevertheless, I am certain that I have genius, and I need not be backward about showing it. I am gold covered with the muck of this world's stupidity. Where is that magazine editor who will wash away the scum of oblivion so that I may scintillate? It does not matter. He will come by-and-by. Until then, I ask you, I just simply ask you, to look at the stuff they do publish!

I try to content myself by speaking, with cool moderation, these few well-chosen words. Yet words at their best, as I said only the other day, in a rather neat little study of a boy that screwed his sister, and then had to cut her throat afterward, words are blurred tags attached to our qualities and to our passions and to all other affairs; and we human beings are like hurried shoppers looking for life's bargains in a department store's dim basement. The first tag that our eye catches we are apt to accept. "Smirt" is a word. People accept it just now. The tempests and the oceans of my genius will end such nonsense.

For words, I repeat, are like shouting in a hurricane, they are like a half-teaspoonful of sugar in the salt sea, and they are like a number of other things which do not at this moment occur to me. I must think up a few more comparisons at leisure. I must not, you understand, speak rashly about words, merely because I happen to be a master of words. *Noblesse oblige.*

For I am a real writer. I do not write for school girls, or truck drivers, or grocers. I write for the elect few. It may be that you, Smirt, think that I am a flickering light doomed to expire without hardly casting a shadow, without ever finding a suitably appreciative audience. I do not concede that.

To the contrary, when I listen to the subconscious Me which is my genius, then I pity you, Smirt, for I know that I shall ultimately write much better than Smirt has ever written, and that I shall see into life more deeply, and feel life more sensitively, and react to life's horror and vileness with, as it were, a far wider gamut of overtones. My work will be more strong and virile than is the filigree fiddling of Smirt, because my superb and forthright work will be a love child, a very lusty bastard begotten upon realism with the phallus of agony.

Oh, I do not mince matters. I say "bastard" and "phallus" right out, with the boldness of self-assured genius. You have already heard me say "bitches" and "whore"; and I say all sorts of other startling things. My titanic and lascivious utterance abounds in many such discordant chords. And, far from destroying its symmetry, they bind all yet more tightly together.

As I told a girl only last night, when we were playing stink finger, and talking about Me, my intrepid indecencies are like mortar mixed with ambrosia, binding together blocks of translucent alabaster. For these things just come to me; just all of a sudden I can feel the repressed energy of my genius flare with gigantic sunbursts of cosmic power, and then I say things like "bitches" and "whore." I do not really have to invent these things.

It follows, Smirt, that very soon I shall have a story accepted by one or another magazine: my genius will thus find its suitably appreciative audience; and then Smirt will be quite forgotten, you big piss-ass, because of his fundamental venality.

* *

FORTY-SEVEN

WHICH REFLECTS FRANKLY

*

Now when the untidy young man had finished speaking, he went away, picking at his nose, and using the proceeds thriftily. And **Smirt** shrugged his shoulders.

"Dear me," said Smirt, "but what an extremely blatant and unprepossessing person is my heir presumptive, with his demands for a suitably appreciative audience! I was not ever, I believe, not ever quite like that. Still, one does catch the resemblance. . .Yes, it very well may be that my dream is now making bold to imply a somewhat impudent moral. So I cry a fig for all dreams!"

Nevertheless, the intrusion of this boy bothered him. Smirt seemed to be finding everywhere in his dream, like a vague and undesirable permeation, the auctorial temperament. It had seeped, as one might say, from the All-Highest to Company and to the bungling Stewards, descending thence to the lowest

possible point, to its nadir, in this lewd and loud-
mouthed and wholly unpleasant stripling...Yet the
boy—that was the odd part—might possess his quota
of genius, after all.

"Each one of us," Smirt reflected, generously,
"must go through this pimply and autopathic stage,
in some form or another, at the beginning of every
æsthetic career."

Afterward one learned, more or less, how to produce one's own notion of art in a manner somewhat
farther removed from rebellion and blatancy. One
became, it might be, urbane. The trouble was—and
Smirt admitted its existence frankly—that nobody's
notion of art was intelligent save only Smirt's notion.

So did Smirt, very reluctantly, see himself as a
small lonely island of intelligence, about which
lapped an unfathomable and unending and uncon-
querable ocean of stupidity. The varying notions of
All-Highest & Company, of the Stewards, and now of
this loathsome boy, had displayed, rather pathetically,
an earnest desire to penetrate the secrets of creative
art, in the same instant that these notions proved each
of these persons to lack the needful ability. Smirt—
and he must face the fact bravely—was an unparalleled genius, to whom all other creative artists were
abysmally inferior; and for whom nowhere in the

universe was there a suitable audience, or even a worthy disciple.

"Well, and what follows?" Smirt said, with unshaken courage. "The thought is not strange to me."

Indeed, this thought had come to him upon several occasions (he could now recall) during his recent stay on Earth, in the time when Smirt was writing his elaborated and jewel-colored prose, of a sort, as Smirt very slowly learned, which was not any longer appreciated, or in fact quite understood, by most of Earth's literate persons. . .For a quaint heresy had sprung up among human creatures, somehow. They believed that prose, howsover magically constructed, was only a vehicle, a species of trash wagon, meant to convey such rubbish as were human ideas, from the author's mind to the mind of his reader. Yet no human idea, Smirt reflected, was either truthful or of any lasting use, because human ideas were evolved, of necessity, by man's fallible mind from the data misreported by man's inadequate senses: all human ideas were perceived, by-and-by, to be ephemeral: and the artist who for his medium employed human ideas, it mattered not of what nature, was but a sculptor who modelled in snow.

"That at least is my idea," said Smirt; "and as a merely human idea, it is of course neither truthful nor of any lasting use. Yet I have always found it an

287

agreeable plaything...The sole trouble is that upon Earth I have found no fitting playfellow—just as, upon Earth also, I have found no suitable audience and no worthy disciple."

He shrugged, saying again, "Well, and what follows?"

It followed that Smirt, the supreme god of at any rate one planet, must henceforward be content to have Smirt as his limited but his truly appreciative audience. And Smirt accepted this state of affairs with his usual modesty.

For upon Earth his rather adroitly written books yet existed, as superb and ever-living relics of Smirt's career as a human being. Upon Earth he had won, at least, his immortal glory, as a tangible prize in the prolonged game played against time and accident and one's own frailty: to perceive this must content, and it did content Smirt, as went terrestrial matters. So his quest thereamong was finished, to Smirt's tolerable satisfaction: and he demanded no more of Earth.

But supernally he would, no doubt, go much farther. That was the present issue which now awaited, docilely, the decision of Smirt, the supreme god of at any rate one planet, of Smirt who remained omnipotent, within limits.

*   *

FORTY-EIGHT

THE SPIDER MOVES IN

*

Smirt stood alone in the home of the Shining Ones. He had already looked over the ramparts of Amit at the busy planet of which Smirt was now sole over-lord. Mrs. B. F. Zogbaum, he perceived, had returned from visiting her parents at Galax, after having been the recipient of much flattering social attention dur-ing week-end stay in city. Threats of ultimatum loomed; wheat was down nine cents, and State Solons convened Tuesday; old Sol was on rampage, and tor-rid weather held its grip throughout West; striker was slain & several hurt in mine clashes; Jap chiefs were offering big arms budget; and, in Chicago, outlaws met doom in machine gun battle with 50 police, Mayor issues statement.

All, in brief, was very much as it had been before Smirt entered Amit, now that human living had re-turned to its confused and threadbare and highly im-probable realism. It was a spectacle before which

Smirt shook his divine head affably; for a god must not be unurbanely severe with the small toys of his whim: yet, as an artist, he would most certainly have to see to it there were many witty and fanciful and erudite changes made everywhere in that planet during its forthcoming régime of monotheism.

Meanwhile Smirt stood alone in the palace of Arathron. Dust gathered there, and in the gods' council chamber the spider was at her work, with the unhurried businesslike air of one who comprehended just how much needed to be done hereabouts before this place could be made presentable to destruction and a fit home for her young.

"A good day to you, Mrs. Arachnomorpha," said Smirt, "and a never ending line of husbands! But is it necessary that Smirt's heaven should be hung with your cobwebs?"

The spider regarded him with eight simple eyes, and replied in frank astonishment:

"This is strange. I do not quite know what to make of this. In all my life, Smirt, you are the first man who has ever spoken to me."

"In these days, ma'am, very many persons tend to neglect these lesser courtesies. But I, none the less, I continue to foster the urbane."

"The fact does you credit," said the spider. "Yet I do not think that I know you, Smirt, nor you me.

And a widow, which I happen to be at just this present moment, has to be careful—"

"To the contrary, ma'am, I do know you, for I recognized you, at first glance, by your fine air of aristocracy. And what, to be sure, could be more natural
than is this *je ne sais quoi?* For you come of the old
race of Trilobites, who lived in the prehistoric
oceans. There is no old Southern family who can
compare with your family, ma'am, for you are an
arachnid of the order Araneæ, of the sub-order
Opisthatheæ, and of the tribe Arachnomorpha."

"These are fine words, Smirt. But how can I be
certain that I deserve all these handsome compliments?"

"Because, ma'am, the plane of the articulation of
your mandibles is horizontal. Your fangs close almost transversely inwards. And your coxal glands
open on the third somite of the cephalothorax. Such
proofs are indisputable. They are scientific; and they
establish your family beyond question."

The spider silently made a little chewing motion
before replying.

"There may be," the spider admitted, "something
in what you say. But to me it sounds like male talk;
and in that there is only a craziness and a bluster and
a squealing."

"Ah, but, Mrs. Arachnomorpha, let us not raise any

question of sex! For in love you do not figure to advantage."

"Where is this love?" asked the spider; "and when was I ever in it?"

"Love is the soul's awakening, ma'am; it is the revealment of the divine nature which survives somehow in all human beings; it is the attainment of supreme felicity; and it is a number of other fine things. It is also the preliminary step to having children."

"Oh, that! Now I can understand you, Smirt. But if you meant so-and-so"—and the spider named this conjunction with the explicitness of a privy wall— "then why did you not say it sensibly, instead of talking so much nonsense about what you call love?"

"Well, ma'am, there is a certain innate sense of modesty in all male creatures; and we never do quite conquer it."

But what, the spider then asked, could Smirt possibly know about the spider's indulgence in an exercise which the spider again mentioned?

"Ah, but come now, Mrs. Arachnomorpha," Smirt interrupted her hastily, "let us restate the question. Let us phrase it, What can you know about my love-affairs? That sounds much better, it really does sound a great deal better to a Southern gentleman, my dear lady."

"What, then, Smirt, do you know about my love-affairs?"

This was a matter over which Smirt shook his dark curls a bit sadly. He replied:

"More than I find to be wholly applaudable, ma'am. For at love you are sluggish: that is a grave fault in any gentlewoman. At best, your lover can but hope to woo you into a dubious non-resistance of his devotion, by bringing you a fresh fly, which you eat placidly during your mating. And, for dessert, you eat up your most recent husband."

"Not always," said the spider, regretfully. "He is too quick for me sometimes. But then that is a husband, all over. He only cares for one thing. After that, he runs away like a coward, and he leaves his wife without a morsel of food."

"There is perhaps something to be said on both sides," Smirt stated reflectively. "But you, Mrs. Arachnomorpha, are rather terrible. You have no need of intelligence. Art does not enter into your life. You go for months, I daresay, without reading a book, or even so much as looking over the morning paper. You do not bother at all about justice or piety or philosophy. You desire only a home and a hundred or two children. You labor always to spend your life in killing and eating, not out of any malice or any personal greed, but merely in order that you may grow in size and provide sustenance for more and more spider eggs—and so, by-and-by, for your babies."

At that, the spider began again to chew silently upon imaginary food. She said then:

"Such, Smirt, is my maternal affection. Such is my altruism. It is only that I am logical about both these virtues, where most mothers and most altruists are not logical. But I, Smirt, I care for the future of my race, whole-heartedly, and with clear eyes."

"It is that which terrifies me," said Smirt, with unwonted gravity. "You are actuated by those high moral motives such as always make the urbane uncomfortable. You abase us, you bedwarf all artists and their piddling ways. You remind me of those superior persons who write so instructively about the housing conditions of the poor, or about the political outlook in Washington, or about the progress of the Negro, or about the collapse of civilization; and who thus trouble me, week after week, with the knowledge that I ought to take a very deep interest in the welfare of my fellow creatures, whereas in point of fact I do not care a bit about their welfare. I find, in brief, every sort of altruism to be applaudable and high-minded and of profound interest, Mrs. Arachnomorpha; but I find it, also, to be uncontagious."

"Then do you leave off all this male talk," replied

the spider, "so that I can get on with the spinning and the weaving and the embroidery which I want to be doing in this place."

With that, she began to enlarge and strengthen her giant web yet further. And Smirt considered her enterprise pensively.

"I admire," he reflected, "from the very bottom of my heart, I admire the high moral motives which sustain this praiseworthy insect through a career of not ever ending hard work and butchery. Yet I do not share them, somehow. They do not incite me to become either a silk-weaver or an assassin. No; I remain still the Peripatetic Episcopalian. I remain an artist in living also, whether I like it or not. And as such, as a *bon vivant*, I prefer at all times to accept that middle world in which men take no side in great conflicts, and decide no great causes, and make great refusals: setting thus for myself the limits within which the great art of living, undisturbed by any moral ambition, does its most sincere and surest work."

*   *

FORTY-NINE

RECESSION OF THE PAST

*

The spider toiled nimbly. About the golden throne of Arathron she had builded her web, surely and dexterously, so that now this throne was the centre of a vast silken wheel. In the throne of heaven the spider thus sat upside down and alone, silent, swaying a little, and waiting patiently for whatever prey luck might send. Indeed she had done her part; hers was the well-earned rest of the victor in a finished conquest. She had reclaimed this place for oblivion, marking it with the soft sign of her cobwebs, which are the authentic mark of things done with and cast by forever. All Amit was now a part of the past.

And out of the past came many persons. They thronged about Smirt with the seeming that each had worn when Smirt had known these persons upon Earth, in an era very long ago ended upon Earth.

"We played with you, we opposed you, we counseled you, we loved you," they said, in thin voices, "and to-day we live nowhere except in your memory. It has been a great while since any living man recalled our doings. Give us new life, you whose every wish must be fulfilled. The spider triumphs here, spreading ruin everywhither through her high moral motives, and all heaven becomes an affair of the past. Yet you are Smirt, with omnipotence in your pocket. You have but to wish for our renewed living. Let us live again, do you make splendid this desolate place with your memories, so that your old delights and the zest of your youth and the incredibility of Smirt's exploits may revive, and endure forever."

But Smirt shook his head. Here indeed was temptation. His past life, so rich in passion and gusto and scandal, so over-brimming with tender and heroic happenings, was a fund upon which any creative artist might draw profitably. To perpetuate Smirt's past would be in every respect pleasing; and in fact, when viewed carefully, what theme other than Smirt could be esteemed quite worthy of Smirt's employment? For here was a theme at once majestic and interesting and of deep importance to the public at large; a theme as to which his knowledge was unique; and a theme, too, which his biographers would forever mishandle, even until Doomsday.

To set them right, by making immortal all Smirt's past, would be a great charity. Moreover, to revive

these perished lives into which he had entered, lives
which but for him would be wasted, that also would
be a charity; and it was likewise in every way an al-
luring task. Yet, howsoever dear the past, the most
deep desires of Smirt aimed otherwhither.

So he shook his head smilingly.

Then the once famous writers whom he had known
in the flesh all looked at him with aggrieved eyes.
They were done with, these ardent rebels, they who
had flouted, in never so many editions, the Puritan
and the Conformist and the Rotarian, and whatever
else in their native land they happened to think about
when they were typing, throughout the glad days of
their vigor. They had made a noise in the world for
their granted while: then time and young critics and
the public at large, and fame also, had put them aside.
So to Smirt, who declined to revive them, they all
said, "Farewell."

After that, the dear women whom Smirt had loved
came also, in the delightful clothes of their youth.
And if their numerousness might just at first appear
a little perturbing, yet was their tact wonderful; for
they seemed not to notice one another, they seemed
not to have been comparing notes; and they came to
him, not at all as the cohabitation of their parents
had made them in crude human flesh, but far more
radiantly did they approach Smirt, each one of them

bedazzling him with some special loveliness such as Smirt's own fancy had invented for this woman to wear in his eyes, and in Smirt's heart also, throughout the term of her lease. And they each said, "Farewell."

So they all cried, "Farewell!" with sweet and aggrieved voices. But one of these fair phantoms came toward him in a long silvery-colored robe, embroidered with black stars and with black suns and with black comets; and this woman alone did not cry, "Farewell!"

"For I," this smiling, grave woman said, "I am served at all times by the powers of the moon, and by all else which is unstable and false and feeble. And so, until time ends for you, and no matter where your light heart may scamper—like a dead dry leaf,—still, Smirt, your thinking will be my kingdom. For my deformed hands alone may bring peace to your thinking; in your thinking my clock ticks relentlessly, at every instant; and my voice is as the wind's voice, a voice which you can no longer understand, poor Smirt, and none the less cannot ever put out of your thinking."

Smirt saw that his own hands had lifted toward this woman, a little, before he clenched them. He let fall at each side of him a still clenched hand, urbanely enough, and yet with a tinge of hauteur; for a sound

logician does not like to be bothered with incon-
venient truths.

After that, Smirt again shook his head smilingly.
And he spoke with some inconsequence, saying:

"There is not any longer in my dreaming a princess. No, Tana; for in middle age we put aside that
remnant of the Middle Ages: one woman becomes
much like another woman: and our hearts are made
safe for democracy."

Then the young college mates with whom his
youth had been shared came also. Each of these whom
time had not slain officially, time had left gray and
unardent. Most of them had bungled their living,
and every one of these boys had died, it seemed to
Smirt, a great while ago. But they came now in the
seeming of their remote youth, just as when Smirt
had known them, when every sort of pleasant and
heroic adventure awaited them, they foreknew, to-
morrow. Hurt and wistful and puzzled, all these betrayed boys came toward Smirt, crying out against
time's coarsening touch, and against the infamies of
being reputable, and against the sure ruin of not
being reputable, and against inescapable death also.
Then they all said, "Farewell."

And the great-natured and kindly persons whom
Smirt had known in his childhood, these likewise
looked at him now, with the high-up faces of grown

people, who were incomprehensible beings, but who protected you from every sort of ill, even from strange dogs and lightning, and who made living a safe and unchanging affair for a little boy. And they too said, "Farewell."

Then there was only the first of all his memories, in the coffee-colored, thin and gray-haired face of his nurse. But this Negro woman's face he could not well see, because of the tears in his eyes. And she said, "Farewell."

So was Smirt rid of his past. He would not ever again, he reflected, think about the dead persons whom he had known and about how little their lives had mattered. He would not, he assured himself, any longer remember that he had entered intimately into a great many lives, as wholly done with to-day as was the living of Hannibal or of Hector, and had thus seen what kindly and laborious and trivial doings appeared to consume the main part of every human existence fritteringly. He would not need to bother any more about the amiable futility of mankind. Instead, at long last, Smirt had forever put aside that forever plaguing thought. He was very well rid of his past.

He was rid of it now that from his pocket he took the forty reis piece, and now that he spoke his wish, because at that instant a large deal which he had known upon Earth, and many of Earth's creatures whom he had loved, went away from him, visibly, like thinning mists. And the spider also had disappeared, for now, in the spider's place, at the centre of the great silken snare spread everywhither about the gold throne of heaven, sat the young girl Arachne.

"You have behaved very foolishly," she said, without any marked displeasure.

And to that he replied conclusively, saying,—

"I am Smirt."

* *

FIFTY

THE DREAM AND THE BUSINESS

*

He trembled; he pulsed very joyously with fine juvenile ardors. Never had Smirt imagined any being more dear than was this girl Arachne, seated there at the centre of the vast spider web which spread out into all quarters of heaven. He came toward her, in a state of emotion which surprised Smirt, and which delighted him too, for he had not hoped to recapture such naïveté. He knelt, kissing both her hands.

He said, "From the first moment I saw you I was doomed."

"I liked you too," she admitted—"I mean, just a little."

"I have moved since then as in a dream, Arachne."

"And to what end, dear Smirt?" said the girl fondly.

"To a most sublime end, Arachne. For we two inherit the eternal city of Àmit. It seems quite a cosy place for a honeymoon. We could not possibly do better, I submit, than to become the ruling gods of

this planet—increasing its pantheon at your convenience, my darling. The affair is easily managed, because I am familiar enough, for all working purposes,
with the great words of power which control human
beings. We two would be omnipotent and very glorious persons, with temples and bishops and vestrymen
and sewing circles and so on. An entire planet would
be in our keeping—"

"That is it exactly, dear Smirt. One house and
one man and whatever babies the years may send, are
more than a plenty for any one woman to be looking
after."

And to that dictum, after a little reflection, Smirt
nodded—upon the whole—in approval. For upon reflection he doubted if the Peripatetic Episcopalian,
at any time during his long travels through uncount-
able centuries, had ever lost heaven, in this direct
tangible fashion, for the sake of a woman. To do that
was a splendid, a gigantic feat; and it crowned fittingly a tremendous career. This Smirt, he reflected,
was at bottom a delightfully heroic person: you could
not but admire a person who did things like that.

"So be it," said Smirt. "I shall obey the dictates of
my heart. I surrender to your blandishments, my
dear, just as you do to mine. I am well content to
have you drag me down, from divinity, into commonplace business life and sedate domesticity...Because

304

it is just as I told Company: I do not really care to assume the responsibility of being God. No, it is far better fun to criticize, and to disparage urbanely, the conduct of a world for which some one else is responsible. I have tried being omnipotent—within limits, —and the utmost I have got out of it, until this moment, has been a fair supply of cigarettes and of matches...So let us by all means not become gods. Let us leave Amit, crying our eternal farewell to the lands beyond common-sense; and even in the crude light of everyday, it may be, I shall create for you a new legend."

"But no, dear Smirt, for as a self-respecting business man," she replied, at once, "you would have to do that by lamplight, if you want to, after the babies have gone to sleep, Smirt, because you will be busy all day in the shop, for so long"—she added, with a fond smile flashed upward at Smirt—"as the biggest of all my babies may happen to live."

He accepted this also, saying: "But I stipulate that our shop shall have a small bell that tinkles whensoever a customer opens the door. Upon that one single point I am adamant, elsewhere wax. Yes, with the bell agreed on, Arachne, I will now consent to dream that I become a shopkeeper, a sinew of industry, and a bulwark of the social fabric."

Then the girl looked at him thoughtfully. "So, Smirt, and do you think that our meeting is a dream?"

"I am sure of it, Arachne, for only in dreams is such happiness permitted as I feel at this instant. Only in dreams does one encounter a young person as beautiful as I find you to be. And for another reason, just now, out of the tail of my eye, I saw a spider turn into you: which is a thing, I submit, that could not possibly happen except in a dream."

The innocent brown eyes had widened beyond belief, in the while that Arachne answered him, sweetly,—

"Of course not, dear Smirt, for that is a most preposterous notion."

"So we are agreed after all, you perceive," said Smirt. "And we must necessarily deduce, as becomes a sound logician, that Smirt—whoever Smirt may happen to be—is still dreaming."

"But, Smirt"—and you saw now that this lovely child was troubled—"inasmuch as I am only a part of your dream, or of somebody else's dream, for really you do mix up a person so, then I am not real at all."

"You are something far better, Arachne," he comforted her. "You are adorable. And if only my dream continues long enough, then I who am gifted, willy-nilly, with a great deal of not ever resting wit and fancy—"

"Yes, but, dear Smirt, but, I believe, you have already told me about that."

"—I shall create for you, I repeat, Arachne, if only you will stop interrupting me, a very lovely legend. Then, it may be, I shall put you into this legend, at an eternal remove from my daily life; and with yet another masterwork of romance completed, I may wander into quite different dreams. It is a possibility we should face frankly. For all artists are made like that, my dear; there is no curing them: and of this fact it seems only fair to warn you in advance."

"But no one of these things matters as yet; and besides," the girl Arachne added, with a delightfully sparkling sort of optimism, "besides, it may be that another doom awaits you."

It was then Smirt took both her little hands in his hands, and he said gravely:

"That reminds me, my adored one, that you really must be very careful in the future. About the past I say nothing, inasmuch as no urbane person believes in a double standard of morality for the two sexes. Moreover, I do not object to motherhood, or to altruism either, when it is practised in moderation. But if any at all serious doom were to befall me in this dream, you see, I would wake up."

"Oh!" said Arachne, flushing deliciously. After

that she turned pale, for the poor girl perceived what a trap she had been caught in, by a sound logician.

And Smirt had the grace to be a little ashamed of his artfulness when he saw the adorable child's dismay, and the deep shock which it had been to her to find a husband getting so completely out of hand that she could not ever hope to dispose of him nutriciously. Yet Smirt would make loving amends, he assured his disturbed conscience. He would devote the entire remainder of his dream to protecting and to coddling Arachne, so that she would not really, in the long run, regret his outwitting of her girlish and ill-considered first plan.

Smirt therefore addressed his Arachne with extreme fondness, saying:

"Yes, my adored child, I would wake up at once. My entire dream—including you, my beloved— would then vanish instantly. So pray do let me impress upon you, once and for all, the fact that you must not loose upon me any such dietary doom as you may be outlining, through mere force of habit, inside that very beautiful small head of yours. To do that, Arachne, would but be to contrive your own suicide, along with—need I say?—the destruction of all your oncoming descendants. So I make bold to hope that your maternal affection and your altruism may combine to dissuade you, my precious, from any such fatal step."

"It is true," said the Spider Woman, speaking from a perturbed point somewhere between ruefulness and admiration, "that the dictates of these two virtues must be honored, at any cost. Nevertheless, this is a sly trick, and it is a mean trick, which you have played on me, dear Smirt, by putting me in your dreams and upsetting my whole manner of living."

"All is fair in love, my sweet pet," Smirt consoled her; "and besides, what occurs in a dream does not count. You should not take it too seriously. The one thing which counts at all, my very dearest, is that the dreaming of Smirt—whoever Smirt may happen to be—still continues a while longer, just as irrationally as it began."

"And yet—that likewise is nonsense, dear Smirt."

"Why, but of course it is, my darling. It is life."

With that settled, they left heaven, in order to look for a suitable small shop.

EXPLICIT